I petted his head as he lay close. His wool wasn't as soft as I thought it would be—more like a sweater Granddaddy had that was a little scratchy. But still, I loved the feel of him, and I petted him as his eyes blinked open and shut.

My heart felt squeezed while I was looking at him. He was so little. "It's okay, little lamb," I whispered. "I'm sorry your mama wouldn't take care of you. But don't worry. I'm here. I don't have a mama either, so we'll figure things out together."

Also by Tamara Bundy

Walking with Miss Millie

PIXIE
PUSHES ON

TAMARA BUNDY

PUFFIN BOOKS

PUFFIN BOOKS

An imprint of Penguin Random House LLC, New York

First published in the United States of America by Nancy Paulsen Books, 2020
Published by Puffin Books, an imprint of Penguin Random House LLC, 2021

Visit us online at penguinrandomhouse.com

THE LIBRARY OF CONGRESS HAS CATALOGED THE NANCY PAULSEN BOOKS EDITION AS FOLLOWS:
Names: Bundy, Tamara, author.
Title: Pixie pushes on / Tamara Bundy.
Description: New York: Nancy Paulsen Books, 2020. | Summary: Caring for a runt lamb helps
Pixie gain empathy when, in the 1940s, her family moves to her grandparents' farm and her
sister, Charlotte, contracts polio and is sent away.
Identifiers: LCCN 2019019591 | ISBN 9780525515166 (hardback) | ISBN 9780525515173 (ebook)
Subjects: | CYAC: Family life—Indiana—Fiction. | Farm life—Indiana—Fiction. |
Empathy—Fiction. | Moving, Household—Fiction. | Poliomyelitis—Fiction. |
Indiana—History—20th century—Fiction. | BISAC: JUVENILE FICTION / Family / General
(see also headings under Social Issues). | JUVENILE FICTION / Animals / Farm Animals. |
JUVENILE FICTION / Social Issues / Death & Dying.
Classification: LCC PZ7.1.B8636 Pix 2020 | DDC [Fic]—dc23
LC record available at https://lccn.loc.gov/2019019591

Puffin Books ISBN 9780525515180

Printed in the United States of America

Design by Dave Kopka and Suki Boynton
Text set in Maxime OSF

2nd Printing

For my mom and her favorite childhood lamb, Buster

CHAPTER 1

Daddy burned all Charlotte's bedding and blankets the day they took her away. Her dolly, her books, and her clothes too. Dang near burned everything.

And I watched as my sissy's things—and my hope of ever seeing her again—all went up in smoke.

When I first saw Charlotte fall flat as a flapjack, I wasn't worried. But when I helped her up, I could tell she was sweating out a fever something fierce. That's when Doc Simpson came and told Daddy she needed to go away to the hospital.

That's also when all the grown-ups in my life started whispering every time I entered a room.

Then when I overheard Grandma and Granddaddy on

the back porch asking Mama, high up in heaven, to hold Charlotte's hand, I feared my sissy was plain dead.

And I was plain heartsick.

I was heartsick my sissy had died, leaving me all alone after she promised she'd never leave like Mama did. Even after she pinky-swore she'd help me get through fifth grade with Miss Meany-Beany. And she'd never broke a promise before.

After I spent all afternoon being heartsick with sadness, I come to find out she wasn't dead at all. That made me feel a wash of relief the size of a waterfall.

But seeing how I'm the reason my sister got sick in the first place, I was still plenty upset. Feeling that truth deep down made my insides hurt. And when my insides hurt so much, I wondered if it was because of sadness, guilt, or the same thing Charlotte had. Charlotte would know. She always knew what to say or do no matter what needed saying or doing.

I figured it was 'cause I was feeling extra bad that Daddy and Grandma kept me home from school for a bit after Charlotte took sick. But it turns out that old school didn't *want* me there! Daddy had to go all the way down to Center Street and talk to the head of schools to make them take me back.

Imagine that! Begging them to send me *to* school. I told him not to bother—I'd just as soon walk barefoot in a field of bumblebees than go back to that school again.

My teacher, Miss Meany-Beany, hates me. I know it. Charlotte had her last year and told me she wasn't mean— but everybody likes Charlotte, 'cause she's perfect.

So Daddy made me go back to school.

No sooner did I walk in the door than Big-Mouth Berta, whose daddy owns the grocery store, rushed up to me and said, "I heard Charlotte got the polio! Oh, poor, poor Charlotte!"

And that was the first time I heard someone say Charlotte had polio.

Just like the president of the United States of America! Polio.

'Course that's the reason she was sick! And I practically wrapped up the polio, put a bow on it, and gave it to her myself.

I started to walk past Big-Mouth Berta when she added in a pretend whisper, "Stay away from Prudence, everyone. She probably has the polio too."

And that was my welcome back to school.

Miss Meany-Beany told everyone I didn't have polio. But I don't think she's certain herself, since every day she puts her clammy hand on my forehead when I get to school. And even though I'm cool as a cucumber, she makes me sit, *every day*, by myself in a row of desks only used for kids like Rotten Ricky to sit in when they do something wrong, like let a frog loose in school.

And every day Miss Meany-Beany says, "Class, I'm sure Prudence is fine," but instead they all must hear, *Class, don't touch her or you'll catch your death of disease,* since not one of my thirteen classmates has mustered up the courage to say boo to me. Not that they'd talked my ear off before— what with me being new to the school last winter. It's not that I didn't have any friends; it's just that when you have a perfect sissy, you already have a perfect friend.

That was all I needed then.

And it's all I need now.

CHAPTER 2

It was lunch, and I was eating the fried-egg sandwich Grandma makes for me every day even though I always tell her it's cold and soggy by lunchtime. She reminds me she's making do with the wartime shortages and rations, and since the hens are laying lots of eggs, we're eating lots of eggs.

I sat there on my lonely side of the classroom dreaming of the jam sandwiches Mama used to make me, back when she was alive and the war wasn't changing everything for everybody. I was taking another bite of that cold, soggy sandwich, minding my own business, when I spied the ugliest bug crawling across the floor. But my bug watching was interrupted when something hit me smack in the middle of my forehead. I reached up to touch it—

and wouldn't you know—it was the slimiest spit wad ever thrown at a living person.

Right then, I saw, plain as day, that boy whose name is Ricky looking at me—the boy I call Rotten Ricky (not having any friends here gives me lots of time to make up my own names for everyone). Rotten Ricky had this innocent look on his face, and he even had the nerve to smile at me!

I didn't hold that slimy, sticky, wet spit wad for a second before I threw it right back at him.

It wasn't my fault that Miss Meany-Beany picked that very moment to walk by—or that my perfectly aimed slimy spit wad landed smack in the middle of *her* forehead.

And the moment it did, time stood still. Every single student in the entire fifth grade stopped what they were doing, including breathing. I'd bet anything that dang bug even stopped crawling across that floor.

Miss Meany-Beany turned her head so slow, like she'd just figured out how to turn her head for the first time. That spit wad stayed right in the middle of her forehead like it belonged there. And as soon as her eyes focused on me, the hate shot out of them like chickens running from a fox.

I wanted to run too.

Instead, I tried to speak, except my mouth must've forgot how. "But . . . not . . . me . . . Rotten . . ." was all I could manage.

Miss Meany-Beany's mouth must've had the same problem as mine. "You . . . what . . . why? Closet . . . *now!*"

She pointed her bony finger straight to the coat closet.

But I didn't move. Even though the calendar says it's fall, someone must've forgot to tell the sun that, 'cause it burned down on us like it was still those dog days of summer. I imagined that coat closet had to be over a hundred degrees.

"Now!" Miss Meany-Beany yelled, and as she did, the spit wad lost its place on her forehead and rolled down her face, in a slower-than-molasses way, and landed on her lace collar.

A look of horror flashed across her face, and I knew I'd have a better chance of convincing our cow never to moo again. So I went into the hottest, stinkiest place in the entire school.

I heard the rattle of the door closing right behind me before feeling something land in my hair that fell from the rafters.

I needed to scream right then but feared the laughs of the other kids even more than I feared whatever was crawling on me. I started flapping my head back and forth, but whatever was crawling on me hung on, probably enjoying the ride. Ripping out the braids Grandma had spent half an hour on after bath night last week, I ran my fingers all over my scalp and through my hair.

After I'd worked up a real sweat jumping around in that roasting-hot closet, that crawly thing must've slipped right off. I imagined I looked so frazzled that Grandma would've clucked her tongue at me the way she does sometimes when I'm not presentable.

I finally settled myself and noticed two old desks stacked one on top of the other. If I unstacked them and set them side by side, I could make a place to lay myself down.

So that's just what I did.

And as soon as my head hit the softness of my arm resting on the desk, my eyes shut fast.

But that's not even the worst part of my day. Oh no; getting hit with the spit wad, getting sent to the closet, getting dang near ate up by some mystery bug—all that was bad enough for my day—but that didn't hold a candle to the part of my day that began when I woke up from that nap.

CHAPTER 3

I hadn't the foggiest idea of where I was when I woke; I just knew my arm was asleep from resting on it. 'Course, I forgot I was perched on a couple of desks, so when I stretched, I fell smack-dab onto that dirty closet floor.

That's when the events of the day splashed across my mind like a cold glass of water. And the thought of a cold glass of water made me want one like I'd never thirsted for something before in my life.

So, polite as I could, I knocked on the door, hoping Miss Meany-Beany would decide I'd been in there long enough, never minding how long "long enough" had been.

My polite knock didn't get any attention, so I knocked less polite and then much louder.

I figured Miss Meany-Beany was being stubborn, but I'd had enough. I decided it was time to walk out of that closet.

And wouldn't you know it, that door wouldn't budge.

I pulled and pounded on it. And then I took to screaming like the school was on fire. In fact, how was I to know the school wasn't on fire? "Let me out! Now! Get me out of here!"

But no one came.

After a while, I noticed something that made my heart stop a bit.

There wasn't a sound coming from the entire classroom.

That could only mean one thing: they'd all left. With me in that closet, they all up and went home to their cold drinks of water and family dinners and soft beds.

I was so dang mad I'd rather spit than cry, but something inside me forgot to tell my eyeballs that, 'cause soon as I sat down and leaned against the wall, tears started flowing.

And right between my sobs, I heard the closet door shaking and groaning before it opened.

I jumped up to thank whoever saved me, till I saw it was none other than Ricky. Rotten Ricky.

"Whatcha doin' in here?" he asked like he had no idea why I might be hanging out in a stinky coat closet after everyone else went home. Like he wasn't the one to have practically put me there himself.

I lunged at him so hard he toppled down like an axed Christmas tree, and I'm not sure who my outburst surprised more.

"Prudence!" Miss Meany-Beany's voice rang out and sounded like she was most surprised of all. 'Cause there I sat, on top of Ricky. I stood up and straightened the darn dress I had to wear to school instead of my comfy overalls.

"Shoulda left ya to rot in there," Rotten Ricky mumbled as he stood up and stormed out of the room.

Miss Meany-Beany's eyes were looking at me like I had three heads. "I know things at home are . . . *challenging* . . . but your behavior is not acceptable.

"Right at the end of school today," she began to explain, "I got called to a meeting with the superintendent, and, well, I forgot to get to you first. As soon as I remembered, I ran here, and that's when I saw you pushing Ricky. After he helped you out . . . I just don't understand."

Then Miss Meany-Beany sighed. "You missed the bus. Come on . . . I'll take you home."

"I'll walk," I mumbled.

"Your farm is over five miles away." She said that like she had to remind me where I lived.

But I bit my tongue to keep from mouthing off. Instead, I followed her out of the classroom and toward the front door. That's when Miss Meany-Beany stopped and looked at me.

11

"I'm sorry," she said.

Now, why'd she have to go and do that? I can't stand it when I'm good and mad at somebody and they apologize. And then I just can't muster up any more mad.

I stopped and stared at the floor, but it was getting blurry from the tears in my eyes.

Miss Meany-Beany knelt down to talk to me like I was five years old. "Prudence," she said softly, "I'm sorry I left you in the coat closet. And I'm really sorry about Charlotte. I know how this must be affecting you."

You don't know a thing about me, I wanted to say. But fortunately, my mouth wasn't moving any more than my legs. The only part of me that was doing anything at all right then was my eyes, and I didn't like all those tears.

Miss Meany-Beany took my silence as an invitation to keep talking. "I think we got off on the wrong foot when you came last winter. And then, this whole . . . *ordeal* . . . with Charlotte . . ."

Ordeal . . . trouble . . . affliction . . .

I was tired of grown-ups calling it all sorts of names, as if dressing up a pig in your Sunday best would make it anything other than a pig. I wanted to yell, *My sister has polio. Polio! And it's my fault, and I hate it. Hate it.*

But instead, I just looked Miss Meany-Beany in the eye. And for a second she wasn't so mean. Her lips even seemed to be forming a sad-looking smile as she nodded toward the front door of the school. "Let's go now."

It wasn't until I was on my way out with her that I saw Rotten Ricky in a classroom with a bucket of something, hearing every word Miss Meany-Beany said and probably some of the ones I didn't say.

CHAPTER 4

We never even had a car till we moved in with Granddaddy and Grandma—and really it's their car. Grandma hates ridin' in it—says she doesn't trust cars—so I never much saw a woman drive before.

Had to admit, though, Miss Meany-Beany looked natural getting into her brown Ford. I watched her start her car the first time she stepped on the pedal—not having to step on it over and over to get it started like the pedal on Granddaddy's car. And before I knew it, she was shifting the gears and we were on our way.

It wasn't like I wanted to chat, but there was something eating away at me, so I had to ask, "Why is Rotten—I mean, why is Ricky still at school?"

Miss Meany-Beany smiled. Yes, she really did smile that time. "He helps with some of the janitorial work," she said. "Washes the desks, cleans the floor, stuff like that."

That sounded about as much fun as being stuck in that hot closet. "What's he wanna do that for?"

The corners of her mouth turned downward, and she looked like she was studying the road for the answer. Grandma is always telling me I ask a lot of questions, and I figured that last question of mine was one too many. But before I could say anything else, Miss Meany-Beany decided to talk after all. "Working at the school helps his family. He works for his lunch and a little extra. Lots of people were hit hard during the Depression. Some never bounced back."

She didn't have to tell *me* that.

* * *

Daddy, Mama, Charlotte, and I didn't use to live on the farm. We had our own little house in Kentucky, about two hours away from Grandma and Granddaddy. If people looked at our house, they might not think it was anything special. But they'd be wrong.

It was everything special.

There was only one bedroom, where we all slept until Mama got the cough. I had that blasted cough first, but

I got better with Mama's care. But when my poor mama got it, there was no rest for her, until she rested in peace forever.

That's when I first suspected I was bad luck for the people I loved.

* * *

In our old town, Daddy was the undertaker, taking care of folks after they passed away. But after Mama died, Daddy said he just couldn't do it anymore.

Grandma never liked the fact that we lived in that house. She was all the time pointing out it was drafty and one of us would catch our death of cold.

Guess she was right.

She told Daddy she didn't like her daughter and granddaughters living as poor as a church mouse. But after Daddy quit his undertaking job, a person could argue that a church mouse had it better than we did.

I felt bad for Daddy. He said nobody wanted him. He couldn't even fight in the war, what with him being responsible for Charlotte and me, and Mama being gone. Said he felt "less than"—but I never understood what he meant. Less than what?

I don't remember there ever being an agreement about us moving to Grandma and Granddaddy's farm, but one day last winter there was such a fierce storm and the wind was singing so loud, we could barely hear each other talk. Granddaddy came to our house, looked Daddy in the eye, and spoke like he'd been practicing it. "I'm not losing another."

Me and Charlotte moved that night. Daddy came a week later, packing our few belongings in two old coffin boxes.

* * *

I concentrated on the *thump-thump-thump* sound of Miss Meany-Beany's car until she cleared her throat and began speaking again. "I have to ask, why'd you go after him like that? And why'd you throw a spit wad at me today?"

And for some reason, right there, traveling down Elm Street, it all came pouring out of me—to a teacher! Starting with the spit wad aimed at me—the same spit wad not ever aimed at her. I told her everything.

By the time my telling was done, she was turning into the lane that leads to the farm. I heard the splatter of dirt and gravel being kicked up on her car before she spoke, her voice choking a bit. "Why didn't you tell me?"

I looked out the window. "Why didn't you ask me?"

Daddy was in the field with the horse and cart, harvesting summer crops. Most farms used a tractor, but

Granddaddy says if a horse and cart worked for his daddy, it would work for him.

We don't get much company, so a car pulling into the lane might as well have been a parade coming down Main Street.

Before the car came to a stop, Grandma was walking out the back door, drying her hands on a dish towel, Granddaddy was peeking out of the barn, and Daddy was heading toward the car.

"How do you do, ma'am?" Daddy nodded as he removed his hat. Then his eyes met mine in the passenger seat. "Prudence Ann, mind telling me what's going on?"

Fortunately, Miss Meany-Beany began to explain. "Hello, Mr. Davidson. Remember me, Adelaide Beany?"

"Of course I remember, Miss Beany. Nice of you to escort my daughter home from school today—but if she's been any trouble, I promise to deal with it."

I lowered my head.

"Oh, um . . ." Out the corner of my eye, I saw her turn toward me and then back to Daddy. "Prudence was just, um, getting some extra help today after school—to catch up from when she was absent. Since she missed the bus, I . . . I brought her home."

Well, butter my biscuit! Right then, I'd be surprised if my eyes weren't bugging out bigger than the headlights on Miss Meany-Beany's car. A teacher fibbing? For me?

Daddy seemed surprised too. "Well, I'll be. That's good to hear. And I thank you kindly, Miss Beany, for both the extra help and for bringing her home." And probably because I just sat there in the passenger seat, staring with my mouth open, Daddy turned to me next. "Well, Prudence, don't make Miss Beany any later than you've made her already. Thank her and get on into the house. Your grandma's waitin' for you to do your chores."

I opened the door and somehow managed to say, "Thank you . . . Miss . . . *Beany*."

And I stood there watching her drive back down the long dirt lane, still not understanding why she did what she did, till the sound of dirt hitting her car was replaced with the sound of Grandma hollering that the eggs weren't gonna gather themselves.

CHAPTER 5

Of all the chores on the farm, the one I hate the most is gathering eggs. I can deal with squawking hens flying in my face even though I don't like it, but there's one rotten hen that's worse. She won't move, and pecks if you try to get near her, as if she's guarding gold.

Before Charlotte got sick, I used to trade her any chore she had in place of gathering those eggs. I'd even choose mucking out the stinky barn if it meant no more egg gathering. But with Charlotte gone, I have to take care of those chickens. Every day. I understand it's fit punishment for what I've done, but that doesn't make it any easier to take.

I stopped first at the water pump and cranked the lever a few times to get the water flowing. After trying to be as ladylike as Grandma tells me I should be by drinking from the tin cup that sits on top of the pump, I decided to forget about being a lady and stuck my whole head under the pump.

The cool water washing over my skin felt like a little bit of heaven. For a few minutes, I forgot everything. Didn't even notice Granddaddy watching me till he spoke up, his voice like a song sung low and slow.

"Grandma gonna tan your hide if ya don't get to those eggs soon, young lady."

While he tried to sound as serious as he could, his winking eye told me he wouldn't tell. I sat there with the water and the events of the day dripping over me as I mustered up a dramatic sigh.

"Tough day, Pixie?"

Only Granddaddy and Charlotte call me Pixie. And not hearing Charlotte say it lately makes the sound of it coming from Granddaddy's mouth sound extra sweet.

And then, like the water that wouldn't stop dripping from my soaking-wet hair, my words started dripping from my mouth again, telling Granddaddy the story of my terrible day.

Granddaddy squatted down to be more on my level.

"And then, Miss Meany—"

He bunched up his eyebrows into a frown, his eyes telling me to be respectful so his mouth didn't have to.

"Sorry. So then, Miss *Beany* tells Daddy that I stayed

after school to get help from her. Why'd she go and do that? Why'd she fib for me?"

"Do you think, Pixie, that maybe Miss Beany figured you'd had enough bad luck for one day—maybe for one month—one year?" he said, chewing on a piece of wheat that moved when he talked. "Do you think just maybe she felt bad about adding to your bad luck by forgettin' you in that closet?"

I wasn't sure if Granddaddy wanted me to answer his questions or not, so I stayed quiet.

"You know," he added, "sometimes we decide who someone is long before they have a chance to show us who they really are. Do you think maybe she's just a nice lady?"

Now, I've been told I have a good imagination. It's easy for me to imagine conversations between animals. It's easy for me to imagine I can sprout wings and fly. And of course, it's easy for me to imagine funny names for people. But asking me to imagine Miss Meany-Beany actually being nice, after all this time spent believing she was mean, was too much. But before I could answer, Granddaddy and I both heard the screen door creak open, and out walked Grandma with her arms folded across her chest.

"Now, if you want to see what mean looks like"—Granddaddy chuckled—"make your grandma wait a little longer for those eggs."

I got up and brushed the dirt off my backside and then reached for the basket.

"It's all gonna be okay, Pixie." Granddaddy said that like he was talking about more than just Miss Beany.

I gave Granddaddy a smile so he wouldn't worry about me, but any hint of a smile disappeared when I opened the double doors of the henhouse.

"Twinkle, twinkle, little star . . ." I sang as loud as I could to scare the darn chickens as I waved the empty egg basket in the air. Most of the fifty hens flew off their perches. Not wasting a second, I ran to their empty spots and started collecting the eggs as fast as I could.

And then I looked at *her*: the old fat hen I'd named Teacher, since she always acted like she was in charge of me. She stared at me with her beady eyes and puffed up her feathery chest, daring me to try to get her egg.

I decided I wasn't going to let her win this one. Especially not after the day I'd had.

I knew Charlotte was never afraid of Teacher. She'd march right up to her, put one firm hand on Teacher's head, and reach under that old hen with her other hand, grabbing the egg like it was nothing at all.

That was one of the many reasons I wanted to be like Charlotte. But all that was just a painful reminder I wasn't at all like my sissy. And it was extra painful when I reached under that old hen as fast as I could to try and grab that egg only to have that dang bird start pecking my hand like it was her dinner.

I pulled my hand back, but not before one of the pecks drew a pinpoint of blood. That was it! She could keep that rotten egg for all I cared. I wasn't going to have my hand used for chicken feed. I gathered the rest of the warm eggs and headed back to the house, knowing good and well I deserved all these bad things and so much more.

CHAPTER 6

When Sunday morning rolled around, I woke up and smiled, remembering today was the day I was going to finally get to visit Charlotte!

Right after church, Grandma packed a lunch for Granddaddy, Daddy, and me to take with us on our trip. She claimed she had too many chores to join us, but I suspected she didn't like being in a car for that long.

There's one main road that runs between the farm and the hospital. Granddaddy warned it wasn't just a stone's throw away, the distance he gives most things, but even knowing that, it seemed like we were never going to get there.

I watched out my car window, seeing leaves blowing everywhere and thinking how fast the weather had changed from blazin' hot to downright cool in only a couple of days. Beside me was a brown bag full of Charlotte's favorite oatmeal cookies, and I tried to picture her eating one.

These days, I would often close my eyes to picture Charlotte doing things. I did that same thing to remember Mama, but each time it got harder and harder, and I wasn't going to let that happen with my sissy.

I closed my eyes tight and held my breath even tighter, hoping that might make it easier to see her.

It worked! I let my breath out, sounding like I'd sprung a leak.

I still remembered.

But I needed to see my sissy soon. "Are we there yet?"

"Yep. We're here," Granddaddy joked. "Don't ya see Charlotte standing on the side of the road right there?"

I didn't laugh. "Why is the hospital so far?"

Daddy spoke this time. "Riley Hospital is one of the best in the nation for treating polio. When the county hospital realized that's what she had, they moved her to Riley, where she can get the best treatment. We're lucky."

Lucky isn't a word I'd use to describe any of this. Still, I could imagine Charlotte saying the same thing. She acted like every day was a wrapped-up present just waiting for her to open and see what was inside.

Finally, the empty, endless road began to show signs of civilization. There was a sign for Indianapolis, and soon we started passing what had to be some of the most beautiful houses I ever did see.

And then I saw the sign saying "Riley Hospital for Children." It was the prettiest building yet. If I didn't know better, I'd think it was a castle, covered in more windows than I'd ever seen in my life.

Daddy parked the car and told Granddaddy and me to have our lunch while he went in to talk to the nurses.

I had just swallowed my last bite of fried chicken when Daddy came back with a look on his face that couldn't hide how upset he was. Truth be told, Daddy's never been able to hide it when he's not happy. And since Mama died, that's pretty near every day.

"What's wrong, Daddy?" I asked.

"I guess . . . Charlotte's not up for visitors just yet."

I gasped. "So we drove all this way and can't see her?"

Daddy tried to smile. "No—I mean . . . yes . . . we can see her—just not face-to-face. We're going to go over by the Family Center area, where there's floor-to-ceiling windows. We have to stay outside, but we can at least wave at her through the window. Won't that be nice?" His voice cracked a bit when he said that.

Waving at Charlotte through a window wasn't at all what I'd been dreaming of, and it sure didn't sound like much of a reunion. The thought of one more day of not being with my sissy made my eyes sting. But blinking those tears away, I reminded myself I was closer to my sissy than I had been for a long time. I took a little bit of comfort in that.

We walked over to an area full of empty benches and sat down. Then we stared up at the long window like we were in a movie theater, waiting for a picture show to start. 'Course, lately all the movie theaters had closed down, because everybody was worried about getting polio. Some people say you get it from dark places like the theater, but that's not where Charlotte got her polio. Some people say you can't know for certain where anybody catches it, but I do.

I know exactly where Charlotte got it. And I know exactly whose fault it is.

Just as I was stewing in my thoughts, a gust of wind blew on my legs, making me wish I had on my overalls instead of my church dress. But before I could rub my goose bumps away, a nurse in a white uniform and a white cap appeared at the window. She waved to us and then gestured at someone else coming into the room.

And then I saw her. I saw Charlotte!

She sat in a wheelchair with her yellow hair pulled back off her face, and was wearing a sweater and a blanket over her lap. She waved at us, and I leaped off the bench and waved back, with both my arms over my head. Then I jumped up and down for her, and even somersaulted in the grass. I heard Granddaddy chuckle and imagined Charlotte chuckling too.

Then I stopped and really looked at her. My sissy. My Charlotte.

She looked at me and raised her hand to the glass and rested it there.

How could she be so close to me but feel so far away?

I reached out my hand like there was even a smidge of a chance I could feel her palm. I don't know how long I stood there like that, but my arm was getting stiff when I heard Daddy announce, "We probably should be headin' back."

After blowing more kisses than I could count and catching a couple kisses that Charlotte managed to blow, we got back in the car.

"Wait—we can't go!" I yelled.

"Pixie, it's no use." Granddaddy sounded sad when he spoke. "We can't be with her today, no matter how much we want to."

"Not that." I shook my head as I held up the brown bag. "We forgot her cookies."

Daddy nodded. "Can't forget the best medicine, can we?" He took the bag and headed back into the hospital while me and Granddaddy waited in the car, pretending our sniffling was only due to the cold weather.

CHAPTER 7

When Daddy returned, he started the car for the long trip home. But before putting it in gear, he looked at me in the back seat and handed me an envelope with my name written on it. In Charlotte's handwriting!

She wrote me a letter!

I didn't want to open my letter yet. I wanted to be by myself when I did, and Daddy and Granddaddy must've understood, since they didn't question me.

Holding it close, I noticed something odd about it. "Why does it feel a little wet?"

"As a precaution," Daddy told me, "they steam everything that comes from a patient's room, gettin' rid of any possible germs."

Even though the damp letter felt strange to my touch, I held it gentle on my lap the whole way home, as if I was holding a newborn baby.

As soon as we got home, I jumped out of the car. Tearing through the porch door, I let it slam behind me. All I cared about was getting to my room to read my letter.

I heard Grandma calling—probably to lecture me—but her calling stopped after the sound of Granddaddy's voice. I sat on my bottom bunk, but something didn't feel right, so I climbed up to Charlotte's bunk.

Even without a mattress, it felt right to be on her bed.

Sitting cross-legged, I looked down at our room, imagining what Charlotte used to see each morning. There wasn't a whole lot to look at, just an old brown dresser in the corner, which now only held my clothes. And next to the dresser was a desk that used to be Mama's. Actually, everything here used to be Mama's, which used to make me and Charlotte feel happy, imagining Mama using it all.

I held the letter in my left hand, and with my right hand I traced the outline of my name. I couldn't help but smile at the honest-to-goodness proof that my sissy was still in my world. I took a deep breath and opened the letter, making sure not to rip the still-damp paper.

Dear Pixie,

Hi! How are you? How's school? And how are things with Miss Beany? I hope you are giving her a chance and have found out how nice she is. Tell her I said hi.

Guess you know by now I have polio. When they first told me, they called it "infantile paralysis," and that sure sounded bad! But I was so sick back then that I didn't even care. Then later I heard one of the nurses talking about my bad case of polio, so I understood.

I really don't remember much about how or when I got here. They tell me my fever was so high, I was acting crazy . . . They call it "delirious." I swore I saw Mama then. She looked so pretty. I wanted to run to her, but my legs wouldn't work. She smiled at me and disappeared.

Maybe it was just the fever—but it gave me such comfort.

For weeks and weeks (it's hard to remember what day it is), I was in a room all by myself, called "isolation." I remember my legs hurt so much, especially my left one. I couldn't even have a sheet on it. If someone even touched it, it felt like they were digging a fork into it. Can you believe that? I tried not to cry. But I did.

Some of the nurses here are afraid of catching polio. There's one that made the student nurses from Indiana University check on me whenever my fever was high. And there's one who is my favorite. She's Nurse Margie, and she stays with me when I'm having a bad night.

I was so happy when I finally got to get out of isolation. I'm now bed number two in a twelve-bed ward with eight other polios.

My legs don't hurt as much anymore, but they don't work too well. Nurse Margie promises me I will walk again. She helps me in the pool they have here. It's a pool that is _inside_! Can you believe that? It's warm and really feels good. When I'm in it, I forget I can't walk. But then I get out again.

But I know I'm lucky. In the ward next to me are boys and girls who can't breathe on their own, so they have to lie in these machines the size of Daddy's old coffin boxes, with just their heads sticking out. They call it an iron lung.

I'm lucky my lungs are still working. I'm also really tired. I hope so much that I can see you this weekend and hand this right to you. But if I can't, know I miss you something fierce.

Sorry I won't be there for Halloween. What are you going to be? I remember last year you liked my princess costume better than your clown one, so you can have it if you want.

Maybe I'll be home by Christmas—or even sooner—the good Lord willing and the creek don't rise.

Love,
Charlotte

Yep. My sissy is in a faraway hospital, full of pain, but she still called herself lucky. That's my sissy.

I'd plumb forgot Halloween was so close. We always loved dressing up for it. Last year, we couldn't go trick-or-treating, since our old town decided, what with the war-time sugar shortage, it didn't make sense. We still dressed up and did some fun tricks, though—throwing corn kernels at houses, Ivory-soaping the windows. But never the screens—that wasn't allowed.

It didn't even matter that we didn't get treats because of the sugar rationing. With Charlotte, everything was fun.

I had no idea what this town did for Halloween. But no matter what they did, I wouldn't be wearing Charlotte's princess costume. She didn't know all her clothes got burned. Grandma'd probably tell me to be a dang clown again.

Looking at her letter once more, I remembered Charlotte sitting in that wheelchair with her hand on the window—and felt guilty that I'm the reason she got polio in the first place. That's when the letter started to get all blurry, as I realized I would dress as a clown for the rest of my life if only I could get my princess back.

CHAPTER 8

I was right—Grandma said the clown costume still had life in it, and she had nothing else to offer.

"But it's so scratchy—and too small," I complained when I tried it on.

Grandma inspected me from head to toe. "Does look like you've grown a foot, doesn't it?" She clucked her tongue and cocked her head to one side as my hope grew that she was seeing my side of it for once. Unfortunately, it didn't last. "But with wartime rations, we don't have the material . . ."

Once Grandma starts talking wartime rations, I know I shouldn't even try to argue. But I still do.

"Maybe you could cut up an old dress or something?"

Grandma gasped. "Oh, now I should put scissors to one of my dresses so you can wear it for one day? It's not your wedding day, Prudence Ann; it's just Halloween." She shook her head. "And there's no extra money right now."

"What about the piggy bank?" I remembered the coffee can Daddy put in the kitchen last month, telling us it was now the farm's piggy bank. "Could we use some of that money?"

"I reckon when your daddy said that was to be for improvements around here, he wasn't talking about costumes." She patted my shoulder, which was already itching under the too-tight costume. "This will do just fine."

* * *

So on Halloween, there I was at school dressed as an itchy overgrown clown.

After lunch, there was a party in the gym with paper skeleton and pumpkin decorations and cookies and punch. I was sitting by myself eating a cookie when Rotten Ricky walked up to me. I'd managed to avoid him since that day in the closet, as he'd been absent for a couple weeks. When he returned to school, he seemed quieter—but I figured him to be still as rotten.

He was wearing his usual clothes. All around us stood ghosts and witches and cowboys and cats, but there he was, looking like it was just any old day of the year. I really couldn't have cared less, but I had to ask: "Why aren't you dressed up?"

Rotten Ricky blushed a bit and then puffed up his chest, reminding me of Teacher, before he answered, "Halloween stinks."

I don't know why that bothered me. What with Charlotte gone and my awful costume, I wasn't feeling particularly fond of Halloween myself. But when Rotten Ricky said those very words, I felt myself bristling like he'd insulted my kin. "What do you mean—*stinks*?"

He shrugged. "Just does."

"Well, maybe *you* stink."

He sighed the way Grandma sighs sometimes. Then he looked away from me as he said, "I just come over to tell you Miss Beany says it's our turn to help at the children's table."

I'd forgot we all had to take turns cutting out and coloring jack-o'-lanterns with the first and second graders. But how'd I forget I was assigned to help them with Rotten Ricky?

Miss Beany'd been nice enough to me the last week or so that I'd decided Granddaddy was right and stopped calling her Meany-Beany. But I hadn't changed my mind about Ricky.

"Prudence . . . Ricky . . ." Miss Beany said. "You'll have so much fun helping the children cut these darling jack-o'-lanterns!"

Before I could ask her why we might like that so much,

Big-Mouth Berta practically danced over to the table in her perfect princess costume. "Miss Beany, do you want me to help? I'd be happy to help."

"Berta, you are so thoughtful to ask," Miss Beany told her. "But maybe you can go to the bobbing-for-apples bucket and help there. This year, we're using blindfolds and letting the children use their hand to reach into the water, instead of the usual bobbing, since everyone's worried about the threat of polio." With that, Miss Beany put her hand over her mouth like she'd said a bad word. "Oh, I'm sorry, Prudence. I didn't mean—"

"It's okay. I-I'm okay," I told her, even though my cheeks had started burning and I didn't feel okay at all. Especially when Berta kept talking.

"How 'bout if Prudence helps over at the bobbing-for-apples bucket?" she said. "Seems to me her clown costume is better suited for that job than my princess one."

As much as I didn't want to be stuck with Rotten Ricky, even more I didn't want Berta to get her way. I stepped closer to Ricky. Me and Big-Mouth Berta probably looked like two hunting dogs fighting over who cornered the raccoon. Not sure how long we stood like that, but it was long enough for Rotten Ricky's cheeks to blush a deep shade of red.

Lucky for me, Miss Beany was as stubborn as Berta. "I'll go with you to help you get settled over there, Berta," she told her. "I'm sure your lovely princess dress will be fine."

I tried not to smile too much as I watched Miss Beany lead her across the room. By the time I turned back to the table, a little girl dressed as a cat was hugging Ricky.

"Hey, Betsy! Or should I say, 'Hey, kitty'?" he said, and with that, the little girl began meowing.

"Hey, clown, can you help me?" a voice behind me said.

I turned to find a first-grade boy holding a jack-o'-lantern scribbled with blue crayon.

"Tommy, right?"

He smiled at me remembering his name and nodded.

"Don't you want your jack-o'-lantern to be orange like everyone else's?"

"Why would I want it to look like everyone else's?" Tommy asked, and I didn't have a great answer for that.

As I sat with Tommy, helping him cut out his blue pumpkin, I listened to Rotten Ricky and Betsy, who I learned was his little sister. "Mama says she won't take us into town to go trick-or-treating tonight, Ricky. But you'll take me, right? I just gotta go trick-or-treatin'! I never been before. Oh, please, Ricky—there's a party at church too. Please talk to Mama. Please!"

"Why won't your mama take you trick-or-treating?" I asked Betsy.

"No reason," Rotten Ricky mumbled.

But Betsy seemed to know a reason. "Mama's been extra sad since Daddy left, and now that Billy's in the—"

"Betsy, that's enough. Don't go telling our family business to everybody."

Betsy stuck her bottom lip out in a pout. "I wasn't tellin' our *family* business—I was tellin' *my* business. I can't go trick-or-treating 'cause Mama's sad about Daddy being gone and Billy being in the war. She never wants to do anything, and that's not fair." Tears started rolling down her face.

Rotten Ricky looked like he might be fighting back a few of his own tears, and so I felt the need to look away. But I could still hear him comforting his sister. "It's okay . . . I promise . . ." Somehow in my head those words started mixing with Granddaddy's words about not deciding who someone is before they have a chance to show you.

And at that moment, Ricky didn't seem so rotten anymore.

CHAPTER 9

A cold November wind blew against me as I brought the egg basket to Grandma after school. Wearing my mittens made it safer to get the eggs from Teacher, but it sure didn't make that grumpy old hen any more pleasant. I'd hoped to warm up inside by the fire, but Grandma said Granddaddy could use help with the firewood.

Walking toward the sound of Granddaddy's chopping, I spied Daddy way out in the field. It turned out that Daddy liked working on the farm and was real handy. Staying busy all the time seemed to suit him. It suited him so much that lots of days I'd barely see him.

"Afternoon, Pixie," Granddaddy said, between firewood chops. "How was school?"

"Okay," I answered. "But what's Daddy doing out there? I thought the crops were all done, what with it being so cold."

"Harvesting the field corn. It grows later than sweet corn, and it isn't for our eatin'—it's for the livestock and chickens."

Even though I shivered in the cold, I noticed the beads of sweat on Granddaddy's forehead from all the ax swinging. I began stacking the cut wood in the wheelbarrow.

"Careful there," Granddaddy said as he nodded toward the extra-big pile of wood I was planning to move to the wood box up by the house.

"It's fine," I told him.

But as soon as I turned the wheelbarrow around, the dang thing fell to its side, spilling every last log out on the ground.

The next time, I put half the wood in the wheelbarrow and made two trips.

When I returned, Granddaddy was wiping his forehead with his handkerchief. "Sometimes, Pixie, we make things harder than they need be."

I knew he was talking about more than wood in a wheelbarrow.

Some people talk to me like I'm just out of diapers—but not Granddaddy. I like how he talks to me like I have opinions.

"I suppose I might do that sometimes," I said. "But it's awful cold out. How much more chopping do you have to do?"

Granddaddy motioned to the already-chopped wood. "This here wouldn't get us very far in a usual winter. And this winter's fixin' to be a bad one."

"How do you know it's going to be so bad?" I asked.

"Crab apples," he told me.

"What?" I smiled, figuring this was going to turn into a story.

"Every time there's lots of crab apples on the trees in the fall—winter's gonna be tough."

"You can tell that just by looking at the crab apples?"

"Well, no. I also look for the rabbits," Granddaddy said as he began helping me stack the wood in the wheelbarrow.

"And what do the rabbits tell you?"

"They're fattening up and telling me this coming winter's gonna be colder than Grandma's homemade ice cream."

I laughed. "How do they tell you that?"

"Well, Pixie, if the rabbits are fat now, it's 'cause they know winter's gonna be a long one. When we pay attention to nature, it can tell us a lot. So I'll pay attention and chop a little bit longer every day to get us through to at least Thanksgiving."

At the mention of the holiday, my stomach sank, and

it felt like the logs toppling over again—but this time on me. I shook my head. "I don't think we should celebrate Thanksgiving this year."

Granddaddy snorted. "Now, don't tell me you aren't looking forward to Grandma's pumpkin pie."

But that wasn't it. "Of course I love eating all Grandma's yummy Thanksgiving food, but should we . . . I mean . . . with everything that's happened, maybe we shouldn't be celebrating."

Granddaddy motioned toward the fields. "Maybe we can borrow another lesson from those rabbits."

"Come on, Granddaddy. The rabbits can't tell us to celebrate Thanksgiving."

"In a way, they can." He sat on the chopping stump, and I hopped on next to him. "You see, those rabbits get as fat as possible for the winter 'cause they know food'll be hard to find, what with all the plants dying or being covered in snow. But when those hungry rabbits find a patch of food—don't you suppose they treasure that?"

"I suppose so," I said. "But that still doesn't mean we should be giving thanks while Charlotte's in the hospital and not with us."

"Well, Pixie, don't you think we should give thanks for a right fine hospital that's helping your sissy get better? And shouldn't we give thanks for what we have left?"

I wasn't ready to admit that Granddaddy—and those dang rabbits—were probably right. All I could think of was that each Thanksgiving that rolled around left us with one less family member to give thanks for.

And I didn't like that at all.

CHAPTER 10

Daddy left early on Thanksgiving morning to drive to the hospital to try to see Sissy. I wrote her a letter that I hoped would cheer her up, filling her in on school, Halloween, and the goings-on at the farmhouse. I wanted more than ever to visit her, but Daddy told me that until we knew we were all allowed to go and sit with her a spell, there was no point in going all the way up to Indianapolis to wave at a window.

So while he drove my letter to Charlotte, I kept busy helping Granddaddy and Grandma.

I tried to be thankful, but the entire house smelled of pie, bread, and memories. And those memories—of our family visits to the farm for the holiday, with Mama alive and Charlotte well, and us all baking pies, stuffing the turkey, and laughing the whole time—they grabbed me with a powerful hold.

I expected Grandma to point out I was being ungrateful, with my gloomy mood, but she didn't say a word. She didn't even scold me for dropping the silverware smack on the floor when I was setting the table.

Instead, she shook her head kind of sad-like as she spoke. "How 'bout you and Granddaddy go and take that pumpkin pie to our neighbors? Ethel over there is having a hard time with her husband gone and her older boy off in the war. And while we have less than usual this Thanksgiving due to war rations, I'd be surprised if they got much food at all today." Grandma looked in the stove at the roasting pan and shook her head again. "That bird is taking its time and won't be done for at least another hour, so you and Granddaddy can run over there now. Isn't her other boy in your class at school? What's his name?"

"His name is *Ricky*," I answered, like I just decided that was his official name, and I noticed Granddaddy giving me a wink.

Granddaddy made sure I put on my coat and mittens, but when I pointed out he only had on the heavy flannel shirt he wore in the winter while he worked in the barn, he shook his head. "My skin's old and tough," he said. "It can't get hurt by a little chill in the air."

Walking across the fields, dry with cracked lines etched across them, I couldn't help but think how like Granddaddy's face the fields were. Mama used to say her daddy was born in the fields and he'd die in the fields. And now he was starting to look like the fields. But even with the lines plowed into his face by weather and work, he was a right handsome man.

As we walked, he held the pumpkin pie in one hand and my hand in his other.

The sound of the steady crunch of our footsteps was interrupted by a screech in the sky that sounded like a scream. I looked up and spotted a hawk circling overhead.

"Look there." Granddaddy nodded. "That hawk's trying to get one of those fat rabbits for a meal of his own."

I gasped and shook my finger toward the sky. "Shame on you, hawk! Go away—leave that rabbit alone!"

"But what about the hawk?" Granddaddy pointed out. "Can't blame him, Pixie—he's hungry too."

I didn't want the hawk to stay hungry, but I really didn't like thinking about him making a meal of the rabbit. "Why's it have to be that way?" I asked.

"Well, Pixie, that's just the way it is around here. The circle of life."

Granddaddy watched the hawk fly away—giving the rabbit something to be thankful for. "Life sure is funny sometimes, ain't it?" he said. "Every day's a lesson in beginnings and endings."

"What do you mean?"

Now Granddaddy held my hand tight as he explained. "Two years ago, your mama and Charlotte both sat with us at our Thanksgiving table. I know you been thinking 'bout that too. And back then, we had no reason to think that'd be the last time we'd all be around that table." He spoke matter-of-factly, not complaining. "You never know when *this* time is actually the *last* time."

We walked on over the fields until we came to a clearing where we could see a small white house a few yards away. By then, I'd come to a conclusion about Granddaddy's observation. "When you think of it that way, life's not funny—it's downright mean."

Granddaddy gave a half laugh. "Ah, Pixie. Life's not mean. It's just sometimes too short. It's up to us not to forget that."

"I won't forget," I told Granddaddy. "But it sure is hard."

He stopped and turned to me. "I'm with you on that, Pixie. Sometimes it feels like all we can do is take a deep breath, pick ourselves up, and push on."

Right then, a big dog came charging at us as we walked into the orchard that led to the little house. I'm not afraid of dogs, but from far away, this one looked more like a wolf. A hungry wolf. Granddaddy stopped in his tracks too.

But as the mutt got closer, we could tell he wasn't much to be afraid of. He looked like he hadn't eaten in a while, and when he got wind of the pie Granddaddy was holding, he tried to jump up but toppled over.

I reached out to pet him. "Now, that's funny!" I told Granddaddy.

He smiled, keeping the pie out of the mutt's reach. "See, Pixie, not deciding who someone is before they have a chance to show us who they really are must work for dogs too."

I laughed as I petted the funny dog, who started drooling on my mittens.

"His name's Mud."

That was a voice I knew without looking up. Ricky stood so close to us that I was surprised I hadn't heard his footsteps. "What kind of a name is Mud?" I asked.

"Well, Ma says I named him when I was four," Ricky told us. "Said me and him got in the mud a lot. From what my big brother tells me, I reckon I'm lucky they didn't change my name to that too."

Granddaddy laughed. "Reckon Ricky suits ya better, son."

"Thank you, Mr. Johnston. What ya got there?"

Granddaddy held the pie higher, making Mud jump and fall again. "Had this extra pumpkin pie just sitting over at the house. The missus wanted us to bring it over to see if you folks might kindly take it off her hands."

Ricky's eyes got bigger as he looked at the pie. He looked over his shoulder at his house before turning to speak again. "That's mighty neighborly of you, but Ma says we can't take charity." He didn't stop looking at the pie as he spoke.

"Well, I can certainly understand that, young man, but this here pie is gonna go to waste if you don't take it. Or it might go to Mud here. Could you maybe take it to your ma and tell her she'd be doing us a favor by taking it off our hands?"

"Guess I could do that, Mr. Johnston." Ricky reached for the pie like he was reaching for a first-place trophy. He turned around and started walking away before he remembered his manners. "Thank you, Mr. Johnston. And Prudence. Thanks. Happy Thanksgiving."

With that, we turned to go. And somehow the way home wasn't near as cold as the way there had been.

CHAPTER 11

By the time we got back home, the turkey— which turned out to just be a chicken this year—was ready. Granddaddy finished saying grace right as Daddy pulled in the lane. I jumped up to greet him after Grandma made a show of putting down her fork and said, "How nice your daddy got back early—we can wait for him and then have our meal together."

The minute Daddy sat down at the table, Granddaddy asked the question we were all thinking. "Did you get to see Charlotte?"

"Sure did," Daddy told us. "From the window again. But she looked . . . *good*." He moved his head up and down.

I doubt if Grandma and Daddy knew I saw the look they gave each other after he said that—but I saw it, and

I didn't like it. Daddy's mouth didn't have to say what his eyes already did: Charlotte didn't look good at all.

That took my appetite away.

Grandma noticed I wasn't eating much and took it as a reflection on the meal not being as wonderful as past Thanksgivings. "Prudence, I know we're doing without some things this year, but I think it's worth eating, don't you?"

"No, ma'am. I mean, yes, ma'am. It's delicious. I'm just thinking of . . . Charlotte."

And then Grandma said the strangest thing. "I know. I miss her too. Especially on days like today. I miss Charlotte being here, and I miss Katherine. So much . . ."

At the mention of my mama's name, Grandma looked down, and I wasn't sure what I would do if she started to cry. My eyes stung already.

Granddaddy's face was sad, too, as he watched Grandma. "Thelma—remember Katherine's first time of cooking a pie for Thanksgiving? If I recall, she forgot something she needed to put in it?"

"Sugar and flour." Grandma looked up, smiling, her eyes glistening as she cleared her throat. "She mixed up the amount of sugar with the amount of flour for an apple pie she wanted to make."

Granddaddy laughed. "And the apples were so tart that year! But she was so proud of that pie."

"You ate it anyways?" I asked.

" 'Course I did. My daughter made me an apple pie for Thanksgiving, and we all ate it—even if it wasn't the easiest thing to get it down. We laughed about it with her a few years later."

And the four of us laughed about it again. It wasn't a big belly laugh kind of laugh, since it wasn't that kind of day. But it felt good just the same.

* * *

Halfway through our own perfectly baked pumpkin pie, Daddy pulled what I'd been waiting for out of his pocket.

A letter.

I was hoping with all my hope I'd get another letter. I'd read Charlotte's last letter so much I knew it by heart. And my heart needed another one to read and memorize.

"Did you give her my letter, Daddy?"

He nodded. "Gave it right to the nurse—*your* letter, *Grandma's* letter, and a letter from Miss Beany. Nurse promised she'd take 'em right to her."

I asked to be excused from the table as soon as my hand touched the new letter. Grandma started to say something about the dishes but stopped herself. "Go on," she said. "But I want you back down here in twenty minutes to help."

"Thank you, Grandma!" I jumped off the chair so fast it tottered backward.

"The letter's not gonna disappear—no need to run." Grandma tried to make her voice stern-like, but I saw her smile a little, and I walked as fast as I could walk without running to my room.

Our room.

Again, I climbed up to her top bunk and sat on the wood board where her mattress used to be.

I studied the envelope like it might start talking to me, telling me what my sissy was doing when she held it in her hands.

Closing my eyes, I tried to picture her, but the only picture that came to mind was Charlotte looking sad in her wheelchair the last time I saw her.

I didn't want a sad Charlotte's face in my mind while reading her words, so I shook my head like something was stuck in it and I wanted to loosen it.

I clenched shut my eyes and tried harder.

Then I pictured Charlotte in the henhouse reaching under Teacher to get her egg like it was nothing at all.

That was the strong face of Charlotte I wanted in my head.

I inhaled slow, hoping each breath might help me cement in my heart the words I was getting ready to read.

I exhaled.

Dear Pixie,

Happy Thanksgiving.

I'm sitting in my hospital room but pretending I'm home with you in our room, getting ready to walk downstairs and help Grandma make the pumpkin pies. If I shut my eyes and try really hard, I can almost smell the cinnamon and see Grandma's good china dishes on the table. But then I open my eyes and the only smell is the alcohol they use to clean everything that touches us. And the only thing I see is an empty bed where a girl close to my age used to be.

She's gone now. They won't tell me what happened to her, but I know she's not home celebrating Thanksgiving with her family either. I just know it.

I miss school. Nurse Margie brought me some books to read. Remember that one book I was supposed to get from the library before we moved, Little Women? That's one of the books she let me borrow. I'm only a few chapters in, but it's good. The sister named Jo reminds me of you, especially after I read your letter about almost getting into a fight at school with Ricky! Plus, Jo hates to wear dresses. I'd probably be Beth, since she always tries to be nice but is a little boring.

I've been writing in a journal, too, mostly poems. I'll put one of my poems at the bottom of this letter. I know you won't believe it, but I miss going to school and having homework. I even miss chores and that rotten old hen! Bet even you would miss her if you were in here.

Nurse Margie tells me I'm getting stronger. She even lets me go see the little babies that have polio. I hold them and sing songs I remember Mama singing to us. It's nice to have little ones to take care of, but it would be nicer if they didn't have polio too.

One little girl, Nancy, is two years old. Sometimes she won't stop crying for anyone but me. Yesterday, I gave her a ride on my wheelchair. I spun us around as fast as I could go, and she clung so tight to my neck I could hardly breathe. But we had fun!

Guess I'd better close this letter now. Be sure to write me everything that's happening at school

and home. I miss you so much, but I know I'll be
home soon, the good Lord willing and the creek
don't rise.

Love,
Charlotte

My Poem
Starched white sheets remind me
Of answers I'll never know
Sadness now sits on your bed
Constantly asking, "Where'd you go?"

And sitting there on Charlotte's bare bunk, I read her poem again, wondering how my sissy peeked into my heart and wrote down words I didn't realize were stuck there.

I was still reading it when Granddaddy came to the door. "Look what I got here," he said as he held out a bone from the chicken. "Remember, whoever gets the bigger half of the wishbone gets their wish. Wanna give it a try?"

We both pulled on that old bone till it popped. Hard to say if Granddaddy's half was bigger or if it was mine that won. But it didn't matter. We both knew we'd wished for the same thing.

CHAPTER 12

Seemed like the Thanksgiving dishes were barely washed, dried, and put away before people started planning for Christmas. The first Sunday of Advent, the preacher man began talking about needing volunteers for the Christmas Eve Nativity pageant. When Grandma nodded at me like I knew what she was thinking, I nodded back, since for once she wasn't shaking her head at me like she usually does in church.

But I shook my head after the service, when I found out what she was thinking. "I don't want to be in any stupid Nativity show!"

"Now watch your tone, young lady," Grandma warned me. "It's good to volunteer for the church. And it's *not* good for you to have no friends your own age. This is a chance to meet more people."

I wanted to tell Grandma that me not having friends was good for everybody. Get close to me, and you'll regret it. But before I thought of any reason I could share with Grandma as to why I shouldn't be in the Christmas program, she stopped my words with more of her own. "Plus, you have a lovely singing voice."

Well, butter my biscuit! This was a surprise since Grandma rarely hands out compliments. But when I thanked her for her nice words, she mistook it for me agreeing to be in the Nativity program. She hollered, "Got another volunteer for you!" and pulled me over to a group of kids gathered in the back of the church.

As the crowd parted to let me in, my eyes landed on Betsy, who waved like we were old friends. She was with her brother Ricky, and standing as close to him as possible was Big-Mouth Berta.

Guess the grocery business was better than most businesses during the war, 'cause Berta always had the best dresses. Her pigtails were two perfect sausage curls, tied with ribbons that matched her dress. She always looked nice— and then she'd open her mouth to ruin it all.

I turned to walk away, but that's when the lady who plays the piano at church called over the crowd, "Welcome! Prudence, isn't it?"

That's the thing about small towns. If you want to, you can get to know everyone. And if you don't want to, too bad.

Betsy weaved her way through the crowd of people to stand next to me. "Last year, I was too little to be in the Christmas pageant—but I'm bigger this year."

When she said that, she stood as tall as possible, so I had to agree. "I can see you're definitely bigger," I said.

The piano lady began. "I am Mrs. Evans. I know most of you participated in the Nativity last year, so you already know me and what we'll be doing. To you new folks, we are going to be acting out the story of Mary and Joseph and the birth of baby Jesus. We'll have costumes and some lines to remember, as well as a few songs we will sing together."

"I'd be happy to sing a solo," said Big-Mouth Berta, as if she was doing Mrs. Evans a big favor.

Mrs. Evans smiled at her—with a smile that I didn't think was too sincere. "Thank you, Berta. You do have a pretty voice, but there aren't any solos in the Nativity pageant. Just group singing."

"Can I be the angel, then?" Big-Mouth Berta asked, persisting. "My daddy can get new material for a costume. I remember last year the angel looked dingy yellow instead of pretty white."

I looked around the crowd to see if last year's angel might be there, taking offense at being called a dirty angel, but since I didn't know who that would have been, I didn't notice anything but a few rolling eyes.

Mrs. Evans really did smile this time. "Oh, new material

would be lovely . . . It's been so many years . . . I guess that would be okay. Yes, Berta, you can be the angel this year."

That made Big-Mouth Berta beam from ear to ear, right up till me and Ricky both got assigned the parts of shepherds. The sour look on her face at that news made me grin.

I might've still been grinning in the car heading home from church. Grandma and Granddaddy were having a conversation, but the motor was so loud and their words were so soft, I only heard bits and pieces and it didn't make much sense.

"Ethel . . . those children . . . boy in the war . . . daddy gone . . . Ricky . . ."

While I didn't hear that very well, I did hear Granddaddy the next day when he announced, "That young friend of yours, Ricky, he's gonna be helping out around the farm every day for a bit."

"He's not *really* my friend," I blurted out.

Granddaddy's eyebrows scrunched up, letting me know that wasn't the response he'd wanted.

"Now, Pixie." He squinted to make sure I was paying attention. "Our neighbors are going through a hard time. Their pa left to go find work last year and hasn't been heard from since. The older boy is fighting in the war. Maybe we don't have much, but what we do have, we gotta share."

I wanted to point out that Charlotte having polio and Mama dying might make some people think we didn't have too much either, but I knew better. And even though I swear I didn't open my mouth, Granddaddy seemed to hear my thoughts nonetheless.

"Some might say we haven't been dealt the best cards in the game of life, but it's not about bellyaching over what happened and what we don't have, Pixie," he told me. "It's about remembering what we do have. Let's not be forgetting that."

I didn't answer Granddaddy, 'cause I didn't want to admit to him that when it came to being without Mama and Charlotte, my biggest fear *was* forgetting.

CHAPTER 13

Ricky started working the next afternoon after school. Shook Granddaddy's hand and only gave me a quick glance before him and Granddaddy headed into the kitchen.

I'd just returned from gathering the eggs, so I wanted nothing more than to warm myself by the fire and read Sissy's letter again.

And that's what I was doing when Ricky interrupted. "What ya got there?"

I shoved the letter in my pocket way less careful than I wanted to, but it was too personal to share. "Just a letter."

Granddaddy cleared his throat behind Ricky. "Pixie, would you take Ricky out and show him where the henhouse is and then bring him to the barn in a bit?"

My toes are finally starting to thaw, and now I'm supposed to give a tour outside?

After putting my coat, scarf, and mittens back on, I noticed that Ricky just had a heavy shirt on. "You really oughta wear a coat. And don't you have any gloves?"

He shrugged. "Don't matter none."

We walked across the yard, and Ricky kept at least two steps behind me, even though he could've caught up if he wanted.

"This here's the henhouse. But I already got the eggs today. Does Granddaddy want you to help with the eggs now?" I liked that idea.

"No, he said that was your job. He wants me to build some more nest boxes now—maybe build a hatchery later on." He paused. "A hatchery is for hatching new chicks."

"I knew that!" I said, even though I wasn't sure what Ricky was talking about. He followed me into the henhouse, and right then Teacher let out one of her deep bellowing squawks.

"Wow," Ricky said, and I could see he was impressed. "You are the biggest hen I ever seen."

"Also the meanest. Her name is Teacher."

"Why do you call her that?" Ricky asked.

"I don't know. Most teachers don't like me. And that hen doesn't like me—so it seemed fittin'."

Ricky looked like I'd insulted his best friend. "Miss

66

Beany likes you. She ain't mean at all. She's the nicest teacher ever. She—"

"Yeah, yeah—I like her just fine. We had us a big talk. I think she's nice now. For an old teacher."

"She ain't old. She's the same age as my brother."

I had no idea what made Ricky an expert on Miss Beany, but I was tired of talking about her. "I said I like her fine now. But still, this mean old hen's name is Teacher."

Ricky reached his hand toward the hen, like he wanted to pet it or something. "What's so mean about this here hen?"

But before I could answer, Teacher answered by pecking his hand.

"Ouch!" He drew his hand back. "I see what you mean about *this* one."

I wanted to laugh, but instead I couldn't stop staring. His hand was almost purple from the cold.

He looked at me looking at his hands and put them back in his pockets.

"Speaking of names, why'd your grandpa call you 'Pixie' back at the house?"

"It's just what he calls me . . . Him and Charlotte."

He nodded real slow. "I remember Charlotte. She was always real nice to me. You miss her?"

"What kind of question is that? 'Course I miss her."

Ricky leaned against the henhouse door, a sad look on

his face. I felt bad I'd snapped at him like that. And even worse when he added, "Yeah. I know how you feel."

Too late, I remembered his daddy was gone and his brother away at war.

"I . . . I'm sorry. I guess you know about missing people too?"

Ricky shrugged and looked down as he kicked the straw that covered the floor. I suspected my mouthing off had hurt his feelings.

Having Charlotte's letter in my pocket must've been like having her over my shoulder telling me to try harder to be nice. I took a deep breath. "That letter I was reading . . ." He looked up at me. "That was from . . . Charlotte."

He smiled, and I think he understood what I couldn't say.

And right there was when I started to realize that Ricky and I had more connecting us than just the apple orchard between our two houses.

CHAPTER 14

The next two Sundays after church found me
staying late to practice for that Nativity pageant. It wasn't
too bad, what with the singing and all.

Grandma was right—I was pretty good at singing—
plus it reminded me of Mama. She used to love to sing
and would make up silly songs all the time. With Mama,
there was always music in the house. Being a part of the
pageant was something Mama would've liked. She'd have
probably even been running it with Mrs. Evans.

Mrs. Evans had us all in the order she wanted us to
appear during the spoken part of the pageant, but as soon
as she started to play the first note of "Silent Night," Big-
Mouth Berta ran from her angel spot over to the shepherds'
spot so fast she might've actually flown.

"I'll stand here for the songs," she declared as she wiggled her way beside Ricky, pushing me into the row with Betsy and the other little kids, who were going to be the farm animals. Mrs. Evans shook her head but kept on playing the song.

Big-Mouth Berta was so used to being the center of attention, it surprised me she didn't insist on being baby Jesus himself. Ricky looked at Big-Mouth Berta and then at me like he understood what I was thinking right then.

When Joseph, Mary, and the big-mouth angel practiced their lines, I went to get some water, and Ricky followed me. I could tell he was acting funny about something, but I waited for him to tell me what it was.

I didn't have to wait long.

"I got something." He reached into his pocket and pulled something out, but then he hid it again, like he couldn't decide if he wanted to share it.

Finally, I could see it—an envelope addressed to Ricky from the US government. And then, he handed me the letter. I stood there looking at the envelope while Ricky watched me. I figured if somebody handed you a letter in an envelope, they either wanted you to mail the letter for them or read it.

Since the letter had already been delivered, I opened it up. The handwriting was the smallest handwriting I ever did see, but I could make out the words if I squinted a bit.

Dear Pip-Squeak Ricky,

I think it's time I stop calling you Pip-Squeak, since you are the man of the family now. Seems only fair. Makes me feel good knowing you are there for Ma and Betsy.

Hope Ma is doing better. I know she struggled with Pa leaving—and now me. This is all so hard on her. I wrote her three times but haven't heard back. Did she get my letters? We only get mail here once a month. We can't even say where "here" is. It's a security thing. They go through our letters to make sure we aren't giving too much away. For example, if I told you we were in the XXXXXXXXXX and headed to the XXXXXXXXXX, they would cross it out before they mailed it. Please tell Ma I'm sorry I can't be there with you all. Tell her I promise I'll come home.

How's Betsy? Tell her I think of her laugh often. I think of her laugh mostly when things are rough

and I get scared. (But don't tell Betsy that part.)
Please give her piggyback rides for me and tell her
I'll give her one as soon as I'm home.

Thanks for taking care of everyone. And
remember to be extra nice to your teacher.

Love,
Bill

"Bill sounds like a great brother," I told him as I handed back his letter.

"The best," he answered, folding it as carefully as I fold Charlotte's letters.

We didn't say anything more right then. I'm pretty sure we were both thinking about the importance of holding on to a letter when you could no longer hold on to the person who wrote it.

CHAPTER 15

I found Granddaddy in his chair, listening to the radio with his eyes shut. I cleared my throat to get his attention before I asked, "If you made something for somebody but found out somebody else needed it more, would it make the first somebody sad if you decided to give it to the second somebody?"

Granddaddy opened first one eye and then the other. "Well, Pixie, I'd have to say I got no idea what you're talking about. Why don't you just tell me what's on your mind." He patted his lap.

Even though I was getting too big to sit on Granddaddy's lap, I climbed on up, since this talk seemed to be one that needed a lap sitting to tell.

"You know Grandma's been teaching me to crochet?"

He chuckled. "I caught wind of some of those lessons. Sounds to me like there's as much scolding going on as crocheting."

"Yeah, Grandma says I'm too impatient," I told him. "But I'm getting better."

Granddaddy gave me a squeeze. "You can do anything you set your mind to."

"So for Christmas, I've been making you a scarf to wear when you're working in the barn."

"Thank you kindly, Pixie. But Christmas is still two days away. Isn't that supposed to be a secret?"

"I know." I looked up into Granddaddy's dark-brown eyes. "Every day, Ricky comes over to help outside, and he only has that shirt that really can't be called a coat."

Granddaddy nodded. "I tried to give him an old jacket of mine, but he said he couldn't accept charity."

"Well, I was thinking—a person couldn't turn down a Christmas present by claiming charity, could they?" I asked.

"I reckon they couldn't do that."

"And a person could always make another scarf for the person they started making the scarf for, couldn't they?"

"Reckon they could do that too. Reckon that'd be a mighty nice thing to do."

I looked back into his eyes, which were glistening now, and hugged him.

"You're something else, Pixie."

Grandma sometimes says that same thing to me, only when she says it, I don't think it's a compliment. But when Granddaddy said it right then, I just had to hug him tighter.

* * *

Ricky was finishing up the extra nesting boxes he'd been making for the henhouse. He was so busy hammering, he didn't hear me behind him until I tapped him on the shoulder, surprising him so much he jumped a foot off the ground. "Don't never sneak up on a man with a hammer!" he yelled.

"I wasn't sneakin'. And you're not a man."

He cracked a smile at that, then asked, "What ya got behind your back?"

"Maybe it's a Christmas present."

He turned back to his hammering. "You shouldn't've done that," he said, and continued pounding a nail that had long disappeared.

When he finally looked at me again, I pulled the scarf, tied up in a ribbon, from behind my back.

"Merry Christmas," I whispered, since I didn't trust my voice not to crack if I tried to talk any louder than that.

He stared at the scarf like he was making out whether it was friend or foe. He must've decided it wasn't that bad, since he reached out and took it from me and untied the ribbon. The scarf was uneven, and some of the stitches were bigger than the others. Ricky inspected it, nodding, like he knew something about crocheting. "You make this?"

I nodded, and he wrapped it around his neck. "It's nice. Real nice." And then he went back to his hammering.

I turned to leave, but I heard the hammering stop for a minute. "Hey . . . um . . ." I looked back. Ricky touched the scarf real gentle, like it was the prettiest scarf in the world, and then his eyes met mine. He cleared his throat, but still his words weren't much more than a whisper. "Thank you, Pru—I mean, thank you, *Pixie*."

"You're welcome," I told him. And I really meant it.

CHAPTER 16

"Sleep in heavenly peace. Sleep in heavenly peace."

With the last bars of "Silent Night" echoing throughout the church, the congregation applauded and the Nativity pageant was over. I didn't know you were allowed to clap in church, but right then it seemed like a fittin' thing to do.

I looked out in the seats, surprised to see Daddy. Ever since Mama's funeral, Daddy hadn't set foot in church. That didn't make Grandma and Granddaddy happy, but every Sunday—even in the frozen winter—Daddy claimed to have something on the farm that needed his attention.

But on Christmas Eve he was there.

Ricky stood beside me. Even though, like me, he wore a brown shepherd's robe, I could see his new scarf peeking out underneath. For some reason, that made my cheeks get warm.

The preacher invited everyone to stick around for cookies, and as the congregation started chatting, Ricky said something I couldn't hear on top of all the noise.

"What?" I asked pretty loud for a church voice.

He spoke again, but I still couldn't hear over the crowd and shook my head.

This time he yelled. *"You have a really pretty voice!"*

And wouldn't you know, at that very moment the noise in the church quieted down, so that everyone could hear him yelling a compliment to me.

Now Ricky turned as red as Santa's hat, and I might have blushed a bit too. But before I could thank him, Big-Mouth Berta ran over to us in her angel costume and asked, "What do you think of my voice, Ricky? I mean, Mrs. Evans said *my* voice really is the voice of an angel."

And in case he hadn't heard her belting out all the songs right next to him, she started in again. *"Away in a manger, no crib for a bed—"*

"Yeah," Ricky said, nodding. "You have a good voice too, Berta. You . . . you both do."

Big-Mouth Berta put her hands on her heart like she hadn't just forced a compliment out of him, and gushed, "Oh, thank you, Ricky—aren't you just the sweetest!"

Then she looked over at me with a big fake smile. I tried

to conjure up something that looked like a smile, since I was in the house of the Lord and it was Christmas Eve and all, but it was hard to pretend with the next thing she said. "It must be so difficult for you to be here, Prudence, singing songs and having fun, what with Charlotte being so terribly sick and in the hospital. Poor, poor Charlotte. I bet you feel positively terrible thinking about her, don't you?"

Right then, any happiness I was feeling faded as her words echoed in my head. *Charlotte . . . hospital . . . terrible . . . terrible . . . terrible . . .*

She was right.

I was terrible. And how could I be happy?

Mama wasn't here.

Charlotte wasn't here.

Berta's words reminded me of my guilt, and I remembered I had no right to be happy . . . today or any day.

I ran from the church, not even stopping to grab my coat.

CHAPTER 17

When I came to a stop behind the church, both the cold and the fact that Big-Mouth Berta was actually right smacked me in the face.

Truth be told—as thoughtless as she was, she wasn't half as bad as me.

That's when I looked down and realized I'd stopped in the church's cemetery—by a grave I knew too well.

The wind whipped my shepherd's robe around me with such force, I thought it might lift me up and I'd fly off at any moment.

Wouldn't that be better for everyone?

I couldn't look at Mama's grave yet, so I looked to the left and saw the headstone of her grandma and granddaddy. And next to them there was a smaller headstone, for an aunt I'd never know.

At least Mama wasn't all by herself here.

But that wasn't much comfort.

I shivered as I wrapped my arms around myself, wishing it was Mama's arms that could still keep me warm.

Then, for the first time, I knelt down on Mama's grave. My hand reached out to touch the coldness of the headstone like I was tracing the groove of each letter engraved there.

KATHERINE ANN DAVIDSON

July 1, 1910 – January 16, 1943

BELOVED DAUGHTER, WIFE, AND MOTHER

I left my hand touching Mama's middle name, since it's the one thing we still shared.

I held my hand there as my teeth started chattering, making my words come out in a stammer. "M-M-Mama. I-I miss you so much. I-I'm so s-s-s-sorry—for everything."

As I wiped my eyes, something landed on my shoulders, making me jump. Turning around, I saw Ricky, putting the scarf I'd crocheted for him over me. "Shepherds need to stay warm."

Unable to speak, I looked back at Mama's grave.

Ricky knelt down next to me. "You okay, Pixie?"

I shook my head.

"Don't go minding Berta. She just talks a lot, and—"

"No, she's right. I am terrible. I shouldn't be having fun—I don't deserve to."

Ricky reached his hand out to touch Mama's headstone. "I'll bet your mama would be the first to tell you you're allowed to have fun even when you're missing people so much it hurts."

I tried to stare at Mama's gravestone, but it grew too blurry.

Ricky continued. "I know how mad my brother would be if he found out I was doing nothing but moping around, being sad. He'd smack me from today clear into tomorrow."

"I'm . . . sorry." I was shivering so much it was hard to talk. "I know . . . you're missing . . . your brother."

"Yeah, I am. I miss him every day. And my pa too."

I kept forgetting I wasn't the only one whose heart hurt.

I'd started to ask Ricky about his pa when I heard Grandma's voice. "Good grief, Prudence Ann! What in tarnation are you two doing out here in this weather without coats?"

And before I could answer, my coat was around me and I was in the car, with Grandma sitting next to me, even though she never sits in the back seat. And somewhere between the church and our lane, she wrapped her arms around me and I might have started to feel just a little bit better.

CHAPTER 18

On New Year's Eve, Daddy went to the hospital and finally got to see Charlotte—really see her and touch her and hear her.

That filled me with hope—it had to mean she was getting better, but I needed to hear Daddy say it.

"What was the visit like? What was her room like? What was my sissy like? Did she talk a lot? When can I see her too? Why aren't you answering me?"

Daddy laughed. "Take a breath, Pru. Everything's fine. I wasn't saying anything 'cause you didn't give me a chance to jump in anywhere. It was great to see her—even if she's weak, she's still Charlotte." His voice cracked a bit. "So good to see her."

"Does she sound the same?"

Daddy knew I'd been asking about this for a while.

Our neighbors the Browns have a telephone at their house. On Christmas Day, I begged Daddy to let me try to call Charlotte, so we walked over there to borrow their phone. But between it being long-distance and us not even knowing how to reach Charlotte once we did get the call to go through to the hospital, it didn't amount to a hill of beans.

I just wanted the sound of my sissy to fill my head—her voice, her laugh, even her scolding me.

Daddy laughed at my question, messing up my hair all playful-like as he answered, "Her voice sounds exactly like it used to. That hasn't changed."

'Course that wasn't what I was getting at. I didn't want to admit that every day it was getting harder and harder to remember Mama's voice. I couldn't bear to forget Charlotte's too.

Fortunately, he brought me a special delivery from Charlotte, which was the next-best way to start the New Year. When I took the letter from Daddy—who might've been smiling as much as me at my excitement—I ran straight to my room.

Dear Pixie,

Can you believe Christmas is over? I clung to

all our Christmas memories this year—hanging the tinsel on the tree on Christmas Eve, waking up on Christmas morning, finding apples and some candies in our stockings. It's funny how those memories helped me get through the days, but also felt so far away, like they were just a dream.

Promise me we'll make new memories when I get out of here.

Holidays in the hospital are pretty much like regular days. The food is still bland and mushy. I mean, I don't want to complain, but Grandma's cooking is a whole lot better, that's for sure.

They put up a Christmas tree in the lobby, and I took little Nancy to see it. She was confused and wondered why a tree was inside. She makes me laugh, which is nice, as not a lot makes me laugh anymore.

The other day, Nurse Margie had to come and get me when Nancy was about to get her therapy. Nancy wouldn't stop asking for me because she was scared. But when I held her, she was so brave. I try hard, but I don't feel so brave some days.

I finished <u>Little Women</u>. It was good, but I

didn't like what happened to the sister named Beth at all. Maybe you could read it sometime and we can talk about it.

Grandma crocheted me an afghan. It's pretty and soft and blue. In one of her letters, she said you're learning to crochet. Really? You? I'll believe that when I see it.

Thanks for the updates on school. I always told you Miss Beany was nice. Tell Ricky I said hi.

And, Pixie, stop saying you're sorry. The doctors say there's no way to know where I got polio. It's not your fault. It just happened—just like Mama getting sick and not getting better. It just happened, and none of it is your fault.

Wish I was home to talk to you about everything. But you know what Grandma says: "If wishes were horses, beggars would ride."

Well, I have to go now.

See you in the New Year, the good Lord willing and the creek don't rise.

Love,
Charlotte

I shook my head. Here I'd been worried about forgetting the sound of Charlotte's voice and the way she laughs. But now, even worse, I was learning she was having trouble finding reasons to laugh at all.

CHAPTER 19

Granddaddy and those dang crab apples and rabbits were right about winter. January was the coldest, snowiest month I could remember. The only good thing about it was that school was canceled for weeks at a time when snow shut down the roads.

Before I lived here, I thought winter would be easier on a farm, with no crops growing, but winter makes chores even harder. Eggs still have to be gathered in the freezing cold, and the animals' water needs to be changed constantly, to keep it from turning into a giant piece of ice.

Granddaddy doesn't have a ton of animals, but they all still need feeding and tending. There's Molly, the milking cow; the horse we call Horse; and some pigs who don't have names, since they're raised to go to market. There used to be a mule for helping in the fields—but he died and Granddaddy didn't replace him. And Molly had a calf a while back, but Granddaddy sold it, even though Daddy says the farm needs more livestock. Since the animals are inside the barn most of the winter, it needs raking out every day.

Trips to the outhouse in the frosty weather were awful. At least I had a bedpan to use at night so I didn't have to go out in the dark when, as Granddaddy said, "nature called."

Big-Mouth Berta brags about having an indoor bathroom at her house. I can't imagine an outhouse in the middle of a house, but I guess it'd sure be nice not to have to do your business outside in the winter.

One of the worst parts of it being cold and snowy was that we couldn't even plan on visiting Charlotte, with the roads being so bad.

Guess I surprised myself when I came to realize *another* reason I was mad at winter was that Ricky needed to stay at his house on the really bad days. Guess I was kinda getting used to him coming around.

One cold stretch kept him home for six days straight. On his first day back, I felt like I hadn't seen him in a month. We did our chores and then thawed out by the fire. Since Ricky had showed me his letter from his brother, I decided to share my latest one with him.

He read the letter like there would be a test on it afterward. I watched his eyes go back and forth, moving over each new line. When he was done, he put the letter down and asked, "Why ya think you gave your sissy the polio?"

This was something I'd never told a soul, other than Charlotte in the letters. But now I took a deep breath and said, "Last summer, Grandma told us over and over that someone in Centerville got polio and that they'd closed the movie theater and swimming pool just to be safe. She also heard on the news report that polio might get you if you swam in water that was really warm. Same guy on the radio said it was 'specially bad during the dog days of August and we should never swim then."

"Huh? What's the guy on the radio have to do with Charlotte catching the polio?"

"I'm getting to that," I said. "So it was the hottest day of the year. Grandma had us delivering the eggs to the grocer all summer long. Usually, we'd walk home along Elm Street, but that day it was so stinking hot we took a shortcut home through Mill Creek. Most of the creek was dried up that time of year, but there was one spot that ran deep. Oh, it looked invitin' and cool, and the sun was beatin' down so hard on me, I couldn't resist. I took off my shoes and started to wade in the water. All I was gonna do was wade. 'Course, Charlotte, since she never broke a rule in her life, scolded me plenty about being in the creek in the dog days of August like the radio guy warned about."

I looked at Ricky to see if he understood how awful I was. His expression didn't show anything but interest in what I was saying, so I continued. "I really was just plannin' on wadin' for a minute—you can't get sick from getting your feet wet, can you? But Charlotte wasn't allowing that. She came to grab me out of the water, but must have slipped on a rock or something and fell facedown."

Ricky gasped. "In the bad water? Was it bad water?"

"It felt like regular creek water, but all Charlotte and me could think of was the warnings. We shot out of there as fast as we could and swore we wouldn't tell what happened. Two weeks later, she got the fever. So you see, it's all my fault Charlotte got polio."

"But you can't be sure."

Except I was as sure of that as I was sure of the fact that I was staring at a blazing fire right then. I stared so long it must've burned my eyes, 'cause all of a sudden, tears fell down my cheeks. Then I got to shivering so bad my whole body shook.

"Are you cold?" Ricky asked. "It's nice and warm right here. Kinda too warm."

I shivered again.

Come to find out my burning eyes and shivering were the start of a fever.

And just like that, I knew polio finally got me too.

CHAPTER 20

I wasn't the only one who feared it was my turn to get really sick.

When Grandma felt my forehead, I saw in her eyes the same worry I was feeling. "I reckon you're warm all right," she said, nodding, her lips pursed tight together. "Ricky, I think you oughta be headin' home 'bout now. Tell your mama I'll check in with her tomorrow."

He stood up. "Pixie's gonna be okay, right?"

Grandma's lips found a smile this time. "'Course she will be. Probably a silly cold or something. Don't worry. Tell your mama hi."

But as soon as Ricky left, Grandma didn't look as certain as she put her hand on my forehead again, followed by her lips. "Hmm . . . let me get the thermometer."

I wrinkled my nose, since that thermometer always tasted of the bitter alcohol it sat in between uses. But before I could protest, Grandma was back and shaking the thermometer down. "Open up, now."

The cool glass warmed fast under my hot tongue. I couldn't even think about the bitter taste, since I was watching the worry in Grandma's eyes. And I couldn't quiet the worries in my own head.

Is this my turn?

Will they be taking me to the hospital tonight?

Grandma sensed my worry. "You'll be fine. Just fine." She put her arm around me and squeezed me tight.

Then she pulled the thermometer out of my mouth and tipped it to read where the red line stopped. Her face couldn't hide her reaction. "Let's get you into bed so you can get some rest."

"What's my temperature?" I asked.

"Never you mind that. You'll be fine," she said again, but this time I wasn't sure which one of us she was trying to convince.

* * *

Grandma tucked me into bed while Daddy went to the Browns' house to call Doc Simpson. My eyes felt so heavy I had a hard time keeping them open, but still I couldn't sleep.

Daddy came up to see me when he got back. "How're you doing?" he asked, touching the top of my head, his hands ice-cold.

"Not good."

He sat on the edge of my bed. "I know what you're thinking, and I want you to know that Doc Simpson said polio doesn't spread much during the winter and you definitely couldn't catch it from Charlotte five months earlier. He said for us to keep an eye on you, and he'll be out tomorrow to check in on you."

That night, tired and achy as I was, I tossed and turned. Grandma stayed with me, putting cool, wet towels on my forehead.

By the weak light of the moon, I could see her in the rocking chair she'd moved into my room, with her head down. I guessed her to be asleep, but I had to tell her nonetheless. "I deserve to get polio."

Grandma didn't move her head, but her words came out louder than a whisper. "Don't talk nonsense." Her eyes stayed shut.

"But I do. I deserve to get polio. It's my fault Charlotte's sick. It would be right if I got it too."

Grandma got out of her rocking chair and sat next to me on my bed. I was certain she was going to demand I confess my sins right there. But her face was kinder than I'd ever seen it before. She put the back of her hand gently on my forehead, tickling me a bit when she brushed away my hair. "What's right is that you get better. What's right is that I don't lose another of my girls. Now hush and get some rest."

I think I finally slept then.

When I woke up in the morning, Grandma was still there. And maybe it was the fever making me what Charlotte would call delirious, but I swear when I blinked my eyes open, Grandma called me Pixie.

*　*　*

Doc Simpson came out later that morning and assured us what I had didn't look at all like polio. And he was sure some bad-tasting medicine would make my burning throat better. He wanted Grandma to keep me home from school a few days, which was fine with me.

For the first couple of days, I think we all worried the doctor might be wrong. Grandma was never far from my side. And on the rare moment when she wasn't next to me, Granddaddy or Daddy took her place.

But after lots of chicken soup and yucky medicine, my fever broke—and I could finally swallow without it feeling like broken glass.

No sooner was I out of bed than I got the best news. Well, not the best news, since that would have been Charlotte coming home. But I got the second-best news I could get.

I was sitting with Granddaddy, listening to the radio playing music I imagined people in fancy clothes dancing to. I'd shut my eyes to picture the dancing in my head.

"You feeling better, Prudence?"

My eyes popped open, surprised to see Daddy standing there, his cheeks still red from the winter winds. He rubbed his hands together and blew on them to warm them. "I'm so much better, Daddy."

He sat down next to me. "Well, good, 'cause I got a big job for you."

Now, I wasn't feeling good enough to do my jobs around the farm. I'd enjoyed the break being sick gave me from the dishes, and 'specially from gathering the eggs. "Maybe I'm not that much better, Daddy," I said.

Granddaddy laughed as Daddy continued. "I'll bet you'll like *this* job. You see, Clyde Grayson has a ewe who had triplets. That's a lot of babies for one sheep to care for—and she had 'em too early. The mama ain't tending to one of the lambs—rejecting it."

"That's awful! How could a mama do that to her baby?"

Granddaddy spoke up. "That's just the way nature works sometimes, Pixie. Sometimes a mama won't feed one of her babies. Sometimes there's no rhyme or reason for it."

Daddy nodded. "That's right. And Clyde was saying he was thinking about killing the lamb so the other two baby lambs could grow stronger."

"Oh, Daddy, don't let him kill that baby lamb!"

"I thought you'd say that. I suggested to Clyde that we take the lamb in and raise it. But it would have to be your job to feed it and take care of it. Do you think you could do that? But before you answer—keep in mind this here's a farm. The lamb would be an animal on the farm—not a pet you get to keep."

'Course I knew the lamb would be an animal on the farm. That didn't matter—I'd still try my best.

But was my best ever good enough?

CHAPTER 21

Daddy moved one of his old wooden casket boxes into the cellar. With the lid off, it made a perfect crib for a baby lamb. I filled the box with old newspapers, a sheet, and some straw from the barn.

Normally, I hated going down to the cellar when Grandma would send me to fetch some of her canned vegetables. It had low ceilings and smelled like mold. But getting the bed ready for the lamb made me forget I didn't like being there. I was spreading the straw out when Daddy came down the stairs holding a bundle in a blanket.

He handed the bundle to me, and I heard a soft sound that wasn't as much of a *baa* as it was a *bleh*. Pulling back the blanket, I swear my heart jumped a little.

He was a pile of white wool surrounding a little tan

face that had tiny black eyes that looked straight into mine. There was a small patch of black wool that made it look like he had a big circle in the middle of his forehead. He was so small and squirming so much I was afraid I'd drop him.

Or was it her?

"Is it a boy or a girl, Daddy?"

"A little guy—two weeks old. He should be bigger by now. He's definitely the runt. He's gonna need lots of milk."

Then it hit me. "How am I supposed to feed him?"

Daddy smiled. "The same way you feed a baby—with a bottle. I'll have Grandma rustle up something for him. Guess cow's milk will have to do."

As Daddy walked up the stairs, I looked back at the lamb in my arms. He continued to bleat like he was telling me something real important. "Calm down, now. It's okay," I said. I tried to whisper soft to him like a mama would whisper to her baby, but he kept wiggling and bleating and looking at me like I didn't understand.

And I didn't.

I put him into the coffin box, thinking he might want to get acquainted with his new home on his own. At first, he was all tangled in the blanket he came wrapped in. It took him three tries to stand up straight without falling over.

Finally freeing himself of the blanket, he stood and shivered like he might never get warm again. I swore he was no more than a wool-covered bundle of nerves.

"It's okay, little guy," I said, trying to comfort him again. "I know you're scared. I've been scared a lot too. But I'll take care of you."

And for one moment, that lamb stopped his shaking and looked me smack-dab in the eyes, like he was saying, *Okay, then I won't be afraid anymore.*

That's when Daddy came back with a bottle, sort of like the ones I've seen mamas use to feed their babies, but this one was bigger than those.

"Where'd that come from?" I asked.

"Mr. Grayson—it's what he used to feed the little guy. Wanna try?"

As much as I tried, though, the lamb didn't seem to want to cooperate. I held the bottle out to him, and he ran around the box like he was looking for an exit. *Bleh! Bleh! Bleh!*

"Come on, little lamb." I paused. "Daddy, what's his name?"

"He's a livestock lamb. Doesn't have a name."

That wouldn't do, but first things first. I offered him the bottle again. "Come on, baby. It's milk." I tried to reason with him. "It's warm and good."

"Try to catch him and squirt some in his mouth," Daddy suggested.

I leaned over the box to reach him, but he was too fast, slipping out of my hands like he was covered in soap.

"I can't, Daddy. I don't know how." I choked back tears, knowing I was the worst person to ever raise a lamb.

"You'll get the hang of it. Remember, nobody knows anything . . . till they know it." And with those words, Daddy went up the cellar stairs, leaving me with a very noisy and very scared lamb.

Each cry of the baby lamb made my heart hurt more than the last. *If Charlotte was here, she would surely know what to do,* I thought. And of course, thinking of Charlotte made more tears come.

So there I stood, crying in the cellar with my crying baby lamb.

I wiped my tears away on the back of my sleeve, took a deep breath, and decided the least I could do was find the little guy a name.

"Here, Lamby!" That was pretty boring, so I kept going.

"Here, Snowball!"

"Here, Baby!"

"Here, Sweetie!"

But the lamb just kept on running back and forth in the box.

"Calm down, buster!" I pleaded, and all at once he did. I laughed. "You like that one? *Buster*?"

Again, he looked at me, and I decided to try once more to give him his bottle. I climbed inside the box and sat cross-legged next to him. "It's okay, Buster. You'll like this."

I wrapped my free arm around him while my hand with the bottle made another unsuccessful attempt at reaching his mouth. Some of the milk spilled.

He licked up the spilled milk in a hurry, as if someone was going to make him stop. I put the bottle where he was licking and tipped it fast into his mouth. His eyes met mine for one second before he started sucking on that bottle. His little head was bucking up and down, making more milk spill out than end up in him, but we were kind of working it out. When the milk was almost gone, he was calmer and sat down next to me. I noticed my hand was bleeding a little bit where his head had bumped my knuckles into the bottle, but right then I didn't care if my whole arm fell off.

I petted his head as he lay close. His wool wasn't as soft as I thought it would be—more like a sweater Granddaddy had that was a little scratchy. But still, I loved the feel of him, and I petted him as his eyes blinked open and shut.

My heart felt squeezed while I was looking at him. He was so little. "It's okay, little lamb," I whispered. "I'm sorry your mama wouldn't take care of you. But don't worry. I'm here. I don't have a mama either, so we'll figure things out together."

CHAPTER 22

"Just what I need—another mouth to feed," Grandma said, letting out a sigh.

Grandma was, of course, referring to Buster. I didn't know—and neither did Daddy—that little lambs like to eat every four hours. That created a problem of what we'd do when I had to go back to school. I volunteered to quit school to take care of my lamb all day long, but Daddy said that wasn't the answer.

That first day I had to go back to school, I got up extra early to feed Buster and to show Grandma what to do when I wasn't home.

I sat cross-legged in the box, with Buster squirming in my arms. I'd figured out if I kept him still, he had a better chance of getting more milk in his mouth. "You hold him like this," I told Grandma as I reached for the bottle.

She laughed. "Good grief! Nobody needs to tell me how to hold a lamb." She whisked Buster out of my arms and held him with one arm tucked under him as she shoved the bottle into his waiting mouth. Buster began gulping it down neatly for Grandma.

"You know about lambs?"

"Sweetie, I was raised on a farm. I know about all animals. Did you think I was born and raised in a kitchen?"

Guess I hadn't thought about it. At that moment, I pictured Grandma as a young girl feeding her lambs like she was feeding mine. Grandma must have been picturing herself doing that, too, since she smiled at him. "This here's the scrawniest excuse for a lamb I ever did see." Buster looked right at her and blinked a few times. Grandma smiled bigger. "But I suppose with the right care, he might have the makings of a decent lamb."

Right then, Buster let out a sound that was half *burp* and half *bleh* and neither of us could keep from laughing.

Grandma put Buster down and straightened her housedress like she'd just remembered she was a grown-up. "Now, let's scoot upstairs so you can finish your own breakfast . . . and try to have a few more manners than this one here."

"His name's Buster," I told her.

"Buster's a fine name. But remember, he's a farm

animal," Grandma said. "He is *not* a pet." She looked at Buster in his coffin box. "Prudence, exactly what is my sheet doing in there?"

"Sorry, Grandma, but I was afraid he'd get cold."

"He's an animal with a wool coat, even if it is just a baby coat right now. He doesn't need a sheet." She shook her head but left the sheet where it was before heading upstairs.

* * *

When I got home from school, Buster was asleep all curled up on the sheet and the pile of straw. I didn't go all the way down the cellar steps, afraid I'd wake him.

Since Buster was nice and quiet for the time being, to show my appreciation for Grandma giving him his noontime feeding, I decided to gather the eggs without being asked.

The minute I walked in the henhouse, Teacher squawked at me with her mean old sound, which started in her belly and worked its way out, like a teakettle coming to a slow ear-piercing boil.

Bwaaaaaak!

"Yeah, I'm back, you rotten old hen."

I turned away from her to gather the eggs of the hens that had scattered the minute the door opened, letting in the icy winds. I'd gathered eight eggs in the basket when I turned around and saw Teacher staring at me.

"Whatcha lookin' at, you mean old bird? Git, now." I waved my free hand at her, and that's when the dang bird decided to do something I never saw her do before.

She decided to fly.

Her flying away would've been a great chance for me to grab her eggs, but there was one big problem: she decided to fly right *at* me.

I threw up my arms to take cover, and all the eggs in my basket went sailing through the air, including two that sailed right back down onto my head.

The henhouse was alive with cackling as another gust of wind shook the door. I looked up to see Ricky there.

"Good grief!" he said. "What's going on here? *Teacher?*"

I was so frazzled I couldn't even answer. Ricky covered his mouth, as if he could hide the big grin growing there. A minute later, laughter bubbled up and spit right out of him.

And as much as I was mad, I had to admit I must've looked a sight. I couldn't hold back my laughter either.

When we'd stopped laughing enough to catch our breath, Ricky helped me grab the eggs that weren't smashed on me or the ground.

"So other than covered in eggs," Ricky asked, bending down, "how do you feel?"

"I'm all better now."

"Good. I was . . . I don't know . . ." His voice was so soft, I had to move closer to him to hear. "I guess I was . . .

worried about you." He was so serious it was hard to believe he was the same boy who was laughing a minute ago.

But I was touched. "I'm really fine. I promise."

"I'm glad." He nodded, but I got the feeling either he didn't believe me—or there was something else bothering him.

I wanted to see him laugh again, but I didn't want to get covered in more eggs to make that happen. That's when I remembered there was something back in our cellar that was sure to make Ricky smile.

CHAPTER 23

The minute I opened the cellar door, I heard
Buster making a noise that didn't sound like his usual *bleh*
at all. This sound sounded like a cry. Ricky stood at the
top of the cellar steps, waiting for me to walk down first.

"Smells a bit," he said as we got closer.

And he was right.

Buster was lying on his side, trembling, and all over
the coffin box crib was evidence that he'd been sick. I ran
upstairs, yelling, "Grandma! Grandma! Something's wrong
with Buster!"

I found her in the kitchen, slicing potatoes. "What in
tarnation is in your hair?" she said. I had already forgot about
the eggs, and when Grandma saw the worry on my face, she
dropped everything and followed me back to the cellar.

"This lamb needs warming up, quick!" she told us.

Grandma boiled pans of water to add to the washtub Granddaddy brought in from the porch. When the tub was half full, I picked Buster up and lowered him into the warm water. At first, he tried to jump back out, his eyes bulging, looking spooked as he splashed water everywhere. I suspected Grandma was worried about him, 'cause she never once mentioned the mess he was making.

I tried hard not to think my bad luck had already got to my little lamb as I swished and rubbed the warm water over his wool with a sponge. Ricky was standing in the door frame, keeping his distance. "You can help," I said, "if you want."

"I don't know." He shook his head as he spoke. "I'm not sure . . ." But then his words stopped, and he came over to the tub and started swishing the water on Buster too.

Grandma freshened up the tub by adding more boiling water until it was almost over Buster's head. At the end of his bath, he looked better and was definitely not shaking like before.

Grandma brought a towel for him and told us to sit by the wood-burning stove for a while with him. "Just till he gets warmed, y'all hear? I'm not turning my living room into a barn."

"Should I feed him again?" I asked before she left.

"Let's give him some time to settle first. Keep him warm

for now. I'll bring the bottle in a bit. He'll know whether he should eat."

Buster nestled down in my lap, wrapped in the towel. Ricky sat next to us and reached out to pet him. "So how long you had the little guy?"

"His name's Buster."

"How long you had Buster?"

"Two whole days."

"Seems like he likes you already." Ricky said this as more of an observation than a compliment, but I couldn't help puffin' with pride.

We sat there, the three of us, by the fire long enough for Buster to dry. He started bleating again, returning to his strong *bleh* from before.

Grandma brought in the bottle.

Buster took it straight into his mouth this time and started drinking down the milk like he was starvin'.

Ricky sat there watching and smiling.

"Wanna try?"

He moved backward, as if Buster was gonna jump into his arms or something. "Nah, that's okay."

But he kept staring at Buster with eyes that told me he might actually want to. "Here." I showed him. "Keep one finger on the top so it stays on the bottle, and the rest just kind of happens."

Ricky scooted even closer to us, and a minute later he

was feeding the last few drops of milk to Buster. "That-a-boy, Buster. That-a-boy."

Buster acted like he might eat the bottle itself if we let him. So Ricky put the bottle down and picked Buster up with both hands. In only a few seconds, Buster's hind legs had tangled in his scarf.

"Hey, Buster, hooves off—that's mine."

I couldn't help but smile.

I sat on my knees next to where Ricky sat with Buster on his lap. He petted him as he kept talking. "Bill would like you. He all the time begged Ma and Pa for animals. They said we couldn't afford to raise 'em long enough to have 'em make us money."

"What about Mud?"

Ricky laughed. "The only way we got him was he come to our house one day and wouldn't leave. Daddy tried to make him scram, but he kept comin' back." Ricky sniffled. "Yeah, Bill would like this here little guy."

"Any new letters from Bill?" I asked.

Ricky didn't answer, just lowered his head to rest it on Buster.

"I bet you get one soon. Don't worry—he'll write again."

But when his shoulders started shaking up and down, I realized he was crying into my lamb.

Sitting there, I didn't know what to say. So after a minute of not knowing what to do, I finally put my hand on his

shoulder the way I remembered Mama doing when someone was sad. We sat like that, with Ricky crying into my
lamb and me holding on to his shoulder, for a few minutes
before Ricky reached into his pocket and handed me a
wadded-up piece of paper.

I smoothed it out and opened it up.

On the top in big letters it read "Western Union." The
first address was somewhere in Washington, DC. The second address I recognized as Ricky's. It was addressed to
his mama and was hard to read at first, since Miss Beany
would've said the punctuation was wrong, but I soon figured out what was making Ricky cry.

Regret to inform you your son was
seriously wounded in France Four January
until new address is received address
mail to him, quote, Pvt. First Class
William A. Reynolds, serial number,
Hospitalized, Central Postal Directory
A P O 640 care Post Master New York New
York, unquote, you will be advised as
reports of condition are received

Dunlap
Acting Adjunct General
1105 PM.

In spite of being used as a living hankie, Buster had fallen asleep in Ricky's lap by the time I figured out the telegram. I kept my voice soft, almost a whisper. "When did you get this?"

"Found it on Ma's dresser. She's been even more quiet than usual lately. Guess this explains why."

"I'm so sorry." I recognized the woeful look on his face as one I'd felt many times, and I tried hard to find a bright spot for him. "At least he's not as far away now. He's in New York."

"Might's well be on the moon. I can't go to New York any more than I can get to France . . . or the moon."

"Maybe it's not too bad?" I didn't want my voice to come out like a question, but I couldn't help it. Guess it didn't matter what came out of my mouth right then. What mattered was what was already in both our heads.

He knew. We both knew.

It was bad.

CHAPTER 24

The snowflakes looked pretty falling from the sky, but when they hit the car, they turned to slush, and the windows started fogging up something fierce. Grandma kept wiping them clean, but it didn't seem to help clear up the window—or her bad feelings about riding in a car.

My window fogged up so much I didn't even know where we were until Granddaddy stopped the car and Grandma reached in the back seat to get the eggs we were delivering to Mr. Green, the grocer. She looked at me. "You joining me?"

"Coming," I said right as she opened the door and the blast of cold air hit me.

"I'm heading over to the grain elevator." Granddaddy kept the car running as he talked. "Gonna see what Emory says about that hybrid seed corn." I understood that meant Granddaddy was considering more of Daddy's ideas for the farm, and that made me happy. The other day, I even heard them talking about saving up the coffee can money for a down payment on a tractor.

The bell on the door jingled as Grandma and I walked into the shop. And wouldn't you know, Big-Mouth Berta was the first thing I saw, sitting on a bench by a window.

She didn't look up as I walked by with Grandma to drop off the eggs, but when Grandma started shopping for her rations, I glanced back at Berta. Seeing a big mess of yarn next to her lap, I got curious, so I moved closer.

"What ya got there?" I asked.

"Nothing," she answered, grabbing the yarn in her arms and dropping a crochet needle onto the floor.

"Are you . . . *crocheting*?"

Berta looked close to tears as she sat back down. "Yeah. I mean . . . no. I'm trying to teach myself. But it's not working. I just don't know how to do it."

And seeing her sitting there so clueless with a tangle of yarn, I started to see her as something other than Big-Mouth Berta. I took a deep breath, repeating what Daddy had told me not long ago. "Nobody knows anything . . . till they know it." And before I knew it, I heard my mouth add, "Want me to show you how?"

She looked up at me like she was surprised I'd offered. I

might have been surprised too. "Would you? I mean . . . you don't have to. But if you're bored or something . . . that would be nice."

I looked over and saw Grandma smiling and nodding at me. So I sat down on that bench next to . . . *Berta*.

"First, you have to untangle this yarn," I told her, trying to find part of it that didn't look like a bird's nest.

She shrugged. "I think it came that way. Gonna have to tell Daddy not to buy this kind anymore."

When we finally managed to get it pretty near untangled, I showed her how to make a loop of yarn to get started and then how to hold the hook. And after a few minutes, I crocheted a chain and then had her do one. Before long, I'd taught her how to do a whole row. Had to admit she picked it up pretty fast.

Her tongue stuck out a bit as she worked—I could tell it wasn't in a mean way, but more like she was concentrating so hard she was biting her tongue for focus. Her hands picked up speed with each stitch.

"I always wanted to do this," she told me. "My mama crocheted me a blanket before I was born. I love that blanket."

"Why didn't you ask her to teach you?" I asked.

Berta stopped working and was quiet for a minute. "Didn't you know?" she finally said. "My mama . . . she died."

"I . . . I didn't know that. When?"

Berta looked me straight in the eye when she answered. "The day I was born."

"I'm real sorry," I said, looking right back into her eyes. "My mama died too."

"I know." She nodded. "I'm sorry too." She started crocheting again, and that was that. No meanness. Just the two of us sitting side by side, knowing there was no need to talk about something sad we had in common that neither one could change.

* * *

By the time Grandma had finished up paying for her groceries, Berta had added a few more rows.

"I think you got this crocheting thing figured out," I said, standing up.

Berta looked at her work and nodded. "I guess I do. Why, I think my rows are looking even better than yours now."

I just shook my head, never minding the fact she was right. Guess there were still parts of Berta that weren't going to make it easy for me to forget my nickname for her.

But then, as I walked over to Grandma, Berta hollered, "Don't forget to get your valentines! The party's tomorrow. I'm bringing sugar cookies for everyone."

I wasn't planning to ask Grandma to buy any valentines,

what with her always telling me about the war rations and times being tough. But I have to admit, after a week of gluing lace, paper hearts, and doilies all over that big box Miss Beany brought in to hold valentines, I'd been thinking about it.

Guess for once Berta's big mouth actually helped me, since Grandma answered, "That's right—you need some penny valentines for your friends. Go pick out the ones you want."

"*Can I?*"

Grandma smiled. "Yes, you *may*."

I looked through some of the sheets of valentines in the store. Some were too mushy and lovey. And some were just silly, like a puppy saying, "Doggone it, I like you," or a tank with a soldier asking, "Do I have a fighting chance to have you for a valentine?"

And then I saw a sheet of valentines that were all about farm animals. The one I liked best had a lamb on the front that said, "Wool you be mine?"

Bet Ricky would think that was funny.

After we settled up with the grocer, we headed out to meet Granddaddy. Berta was still sitting on the bench, concentrating so much on her crocheting that she didn't seem to notice us leaving. But wouldn't you know, right when we opened the door, mixed with the jingle of the bell, I heard Berta say, "Thanks for helping me."

On the way home, I thought about Berta, sitting there all sad one minute and then bragging the next.

Granddaddy always says we shouldn't try to figure out who people are until they show us. But what are you supposed to do when somebody shows you so many different things about themselves you just can't figure 'em out at all?

CHAPTER 25

Even though the sun was barely up, I was already down in the cellar feeding Buster. Today was the day I was finally going to see Charlotte live and in person, and it couldn't happen soon enough.

Last night, I lay awake staring up at her bunk, remembering all the stories she would tell me on the nights I couldn't fall asleep. And as much as the sadness of missing her tried its darndest to creep over me, I wouldn't let it. I only had room for excitement since I knew I was about to see her again!

See her. Hear her. Hug her.

Charlotte's hugs are almost as good as Mama's. And the thought of hugging at least one of 'em again made me squeal.

Buster didn't take too kindly to my squealing and looked

up at me from his bottle as if to ask if I had any manners at all. I laughed. "Sorry, Buster, but you gotta understand I'm seeing my sissy today!"

And as if that wasn't the most exciting news ever, he went right back to slurping up his bottle.

Then it was off to the henhouse for me.

Now that mud season was here, the trek to the henhouse was tricky. With each step, I had to watch where I stomped my feet—or I'd end up on my backside in a sloppy mess of mud and melting snow.

When I finally got there, I glanced behind me, surprised at how different the farm looked this time of year. I guess much of my life looked different too. But today I was plenty happy. And even that dang chicken wasn't going to ruin my mood! I might've set a new record for gathering the eggs.

"Look who's up at the crack of dawn!" Grandma said as I came into the kitchen and handed her the egg basket. "Guess I don't have to ask what woke you today."

It was so early I got to have breakfast with Daddy.

Grandma must have been so happy for me that she couldn't even comment on how I gulped down my breakfast.

But Daddy did. "No need to rush. Visiting hours don't start till noon. Plus, before I take you this time, I'm gonna see if I can make a call to the hospital on the Browns' phone, just to make sure."

I almost dropped the dish I'd started washing. "Make sure of what, Daddy?"

"Now, don't get all worried. It's just a precaution—to make sure Charlotte is still having visitors. I don't want ya to get all the way there and be disappointed—*again*. I won't do that to ya."

"But . . . but . . . you don't think she's worse, do you?"

"'Course not. I got no reason to think Charlotte's anything but improvin'—but I want to make this call first, okay?"

It was not okay that I had to wait what seemed like hours for Daddy to get back.

And it was definitely not okay when Daddy walked in the door and said, "It's a good thing I called first."

"What's wrong with Charlotte, Daddy?" I was fighting back tears, and the tears were about to win.

"Charlotte's fine, Pru. She's getting better."

"Oh, good! Then we can see her today?"

Daddy shook his head. "I'm afraid not. Remember how you got sick a while back?"

"Yeah. But I'm all better. I—"

"It's not you being sick now—it's everyone else. There's some influenza going around, and they're cutting back on visitors."

"So we can't see her anymore?"

"Well, they're not stopping everyone from visiting, but

they are stopping children—anyone under fifteen—from coming."

"But that's not fair. I already was sick, and I'm better, and—" My tears tumbled out.

Daddy pulled me close, my cheek rubbing on the roughness of his coat. "I know, honey. I know you're disappointed, and I'm real sorry. I promise you I will bring you as soon as I can. And I bet she'll have a letter for you."

I just shook my head.

'Course I loved Charlotte's letters, but it wasn't the same.

A letter's not like being in the same room with a person, breathing the same air, holding on to each other. Knowing they understand the words you're saying—as well as the words you're not saying.

CHAPTER 26

While Granddaddy and Daddy went to the hospital, Grandma thought it'd be good for me to stay busy. I'm not sure why so many of the things that are good for me are not at all fun for me.

But since my perfect day was already ruined, it seemed only fitting to have to sort through buckets of potatoes that smelled like dirt, finding the ones ready for planting. My job—and Betsy's job, too, since she'd been tagging along with Ricky more and more—was to find the potatoes just starting to sprout eyes and throw away the ones that were starting to go bad.

"Ew," Betsy squealed as her finger poked through a rotten one. She pulled it out and flung the mushy potato across the table. If I hadn't been so mad about everything, I might have laughed at the sour look on her face.

"Do you do this every year?" she asked, wiping her hand on her overalls.

"Sure do," Grandma answered.

Betsy stretched her neck to look over Grandma's shoulder. "What do you do with *those* pieces that aren't rotten?"

"These here will dry for twenty-four hours," Grandma said. "Then, they'll get planted on Saint Paddy's Day, and from the eyes, new potato plants will grow."

"What's special about that day?"

Grandma paused from her chopping for a minute and looked up, like she was enjoying the memory. "Just a family tradition, I guess. Probably has more to do with the timing in the month of March—but my daddy always planted potatoes on that day, so we've always done it too."

I laid the last of the not-rotten potatoes on the table for Grandma, thinking about traditions. I wished things would stop changing so much around here so that we could have more traditions—and people—to hold on to.

I mumbled, "I really wanted to see Charlotte today."

"I know ya did, Pru." Grandma's voice was soft.

"Seems strange to me—a hospital telling sick people to stay away," I said, starting to complain again, but just then

Ricky came in from the barn, and Betsy jumped up to give him a hug as if she hadn't just seen him an hour earlier.

Ricky hugged her back. "You been a good girl in here, Betsy?"

"I'm helping go through the stinky potatoes to find the ones with eyes to plant on Saint . . . Saint . . . *Potatoes'* Day?"

"Saint Paddy's Day," Grandma said.

Ricky smiled at his sister and then turned to Grandma. "I'm all done today, Mrs. Johnston. Noticed Horse's been shifting his weight off one of his hind feet—might need a new shoein' soon. Thought I'd mention it."

"Thanks, Ricky. I'll be sure to pass that along. Wanna come sit for a spell? Maybe talk to this young lady to keep her from traipsin' to Indianapolis to demand the hospital let her in," Grandma said, winking at me.

"Thank you—but me and Betsy better be getting home."

Grandma patted his shoulder. "How's your mama today?"

"She's . . . um . . ." He glanced at Betsy, who was back poking around the bucket of bad potatoes. "I think she'll be right fine real soon. She's just . . . *tired.*" He cleared his throat like there was something stuck there.

Ricky told me last week his mama had been staying in bed a lot recently. A few ladies from church had started taking turns checking on her and bringing food.

But Ricky didn't like to talk about it much.

"I bet you're right," Grandma said. "Your mama'll be back to feeling like her old self soon. Meanwhile, I got some leftover ham I'd like you to take home with you."

"Thank you, ma'am. That's real nice." Ricky tried to smile at Grandma. "Ma said when she's feeling better, she's gonna have to bake from here to the end of days to pay back all the kind folks who've helped us out."

"That's what neighbors are for." Grandma wrapped up the ham as she talked. "Tell your mama her only worry needs to be to rest up and feel better."

"I sure will," Ricky said.

After hugs for each of us from Betsy, they both headed home while we cleaned up the potato mess.

"How much time you think his mama will need?" I asked.

"Can't rightly say. Sometimes the pain we can't see is the deepest pain of all. We'll help her till she's ready to help herself—and her youngins."

"I'm surprised Betsy seems happy all the time."

Grandma's face pinched up a bit before she answered. "I imagine she feels more than she lets on. Things have gotten hard over there—an aunt from Cincinnati wanted to get Betsy and Ricky to come stay with her, but Ethel didn't want to leave in case one of the men returns. She says they can manage just fine, with Ricky being such a help."

I thought of Bill's letter to Ricky, and my heart hurt for Ricky and his family.

"He's a nice boy," Grandma said, but she didn't have to tell me that.

Then, gathering up all the potato pieces, she said, "Tell you what—since we're done with these here potatoes, let's take 'em down to the cellar, where you'll see I'm fixing to finish making the butter. The milk's been sittin' in the milk cooler for three days now, so there'll be some cream on top that *somebody* could have if they wanted."

With each step down the cellar stairs, I thought about Ricky and Betsy and how they must be missing their old traditions and family members too. And still, they just kept getting up each morning, hoping each new day would be better than the one before.

Maybe that's what Granddaddy would call "pushing on."

CHAPTER 27

Mama used to say Charlotte and I grew by leaps and bounds. I don't think I ever understood that more than I did watching Buster grow so fast. As a matter of fact, I worried if he didn't slow down his growing, he'd soon be leaping and bounding out of the old casket box.

I knew it wouldn't be too much longer that he could stay in the cellar.

I loved having him in the house—but I did not love keeping his box clean. Seemed like every time I raked it out and carried the yucky bucket outside, it was time to do it all over again. But I knew the only thing worse than smelling Buster's mess would be for Grandma to smell it first.

I was washing out the bucket by the water pump when I heard Granddaddy and Daddy coming down the lane.

"What did Charlotte look like when you saw her?" I said, pouncing on them the minute they got out of the car.

"Charlotte?" Granddaddy cleared his throat. "Let me see . . . Well, she's ten foot tall now and has blue hair growing all over her head." He swished my hair while we walked into the house.

"I'm serious," I said. "Tell me exactly what Charlotte looked like when you saw her. *Please*."

Granddaddy gave me a hug, and Daddy answered. "Well, Pru, she looked like Charlotte, but a thinner, more tired Charlotte."

"When can she come home?"

Daddy shook his head. "I'm not gonna lie to ya. She's working really hard to get better—and she *is* getting better. But she has a ways to go yet."

Grandma joined in the conversation, and they started talking about her doctor and "therapy" and "support braces" and a whole bunch of other medical stuff.

I took the new letter Charlotte had given them for me and headed upstairs, thinking I didn't like Daddy's prediction that she still had a ways to go before coming home.

Dear Pixie,

I miss you!

How's everything at the farm? I can't believe I'm missing the whole winter there. Remember last year when we first moved there and thought it was the coldest, snowiest place on earth? I remember standing in the orchard early one morning, seeing everything covered with a thick blanket of white snow. I remember it being fresh and perfect.

I want to see that again.

There's a lot of white here too. White sheets, white nurse uniforms, white doctor coats, white walls. Like the snow, white covers everything. It's so very cold, but not very pretty.

It was Nancy's birthday last week, and we threw her a party. I gave her one of my paper dolls and some of the paper outfits I got from Daddy for Christmas, and Nurse Margie brought her a piece of cake from the cafeteria with three candles in it. Nancy had so much fun but was kind of confused by it all. I don't blame her. How can she be one year older when she's stuck in here?

It's like the rest of the world stopped. No more Christmas, no more New Year, no more birthdays. I wrote a poem about it:

> *Time no longer ticks by*
> *When you've only time to kill*
> *'Cause stuck in a hospital,*
> *Time stands deadly still.*

Sorry I'm so depressing. I'll think of something good to tell you.

Oh—I know. I screamed yesterday. Well, that wasn't the good part. Here's what happened:

I've been reading to this one girl, Gloria, who is in the iron lung machine I told you about, the one that's the size of the old coffin boxes. She needs the push of the machine to breathe. She spends her whole day and night lying down, stuck in that thing. Once a day, the nurses take the lid off and give her medicines and massage her legs and wash her, but it can only be for a short time, or she'll die, since her lungs can't breathe in the oxygen on their own.

Well, I rolled in to read to Gloria when I saw the lid off of her iron lung and the nurse talking on the phone at her desk, not paying Gloria any mind at all. Gloria was struggling to breathe, but she couldn't talk . . . She couldn't get enough air to say anything. "Hey!" I yelled to the nurse on the phone, but she ignored me, and I knew there wasn't much time.

I tried to reach the cover, but I didn't know how to hook everything back up, so I did the only thing I could think of. I screamed at the top of my lungs. "Somebody help! Somebody help!" And I didn't stop until two nurses, a doctor, and the janitor got to the room. They saw Gloria struggling and fixed the iron lung back on her. That nurse got a talking-to, but not before giving me a dirty look.

Poor Gloria! She was so scared! And I was so happy my lungs were working fine!

I took three steps today. It was with a walker and nurses holding me—but it's worth talking about. I'd forgot what it felt like to stand. Standing feels good.

I plan on standing at home before you know it, the good Lord willing and the creek don't rise.

Love,
Charlotte

I stared at my letter and couldn't stop smiling.

My sissy . . . *my Charlotte* . . . was something else! There she was thinking of other people even in the hospital—giving a party for a little girl and saving another girl's life!

And knowing she was still the kind, brave sister I remembered made me feel like she wasn't as far away as I feared, even if she still had "a ways to go."

CHAPTER 28

Even though summer still seemed like a far-away dream, one morning Miss Beany started talking about the end of the school year.

"This spring, all of us teachers have decided we would like to have a school-wide pageant to celebrate how hard you have all worked. With the war and rationing, everyone has been through a lot, so we want to do something extra special for our community."

Some kids started to clap, like that excited them too. I just sat there thinking how Charlotte wouldn't be here to celebrate with us.

My mind must've drifted, 'cause the next thing I knew, kids were standing up and moving to sit in different chairs.

"What's going on?" I asked as Ricky and Berta appeared next to me.

"Aren't you a little daydreamer!" Berta laughed. "Miss Beany assigned us groups to work in for the pageant. And we're together."

Ricky pulled up a chair and sat next to me. "Guess I'm with you guys for this too."

"So, what are we supposed to do?" I asked.

Berta rolled her eyes. "If you had listened, like Ricky and me, you'd know that each group is writing a speech about America. Then we will present the speeches to the class, and the best speech from our class will be given at the pageant. So we have to win."

I turned to see what Ricky thought of that while Berta kept talking. "And, Prudence, why don't you go get us some paper so we can write down some of our ideas?"

I really didn't like taking orders from Berta—or having her roll her eyes at me—but anytime I could get up in class without asking for permission, I would.

Right as I walked past her chair, I swear she stuck her foot out in front of me, making me fall flat on the floor.

"Why in tarnation did you do that?" I yelled, giving her the meanest look I could muster.

She looked shocked, and if I didn't know better, I'd almost believe her. "Oh my goodness, I'm so sorry," she said.

"I was just stretching my legs. I swear." She reached out her hand to me. "Let me help you up."

I ignored her as I stood up.

"You okay, Pixie?" Ricky asked.

"I'm fine," I mumbled as I went to get the paper.

I wasn't gone more than a minute, but when I got back, Berta had the whole thing worked out. "So the speech should be about our store and how it has helped everybody during the war."

The way she said it, it didn't sound like a suggestion she was offering, but a full-fledged decision. I didn't really care what we wrote the speech about, but I wasn't gonna let her boss me.

"I don't know," I said, watching where I walked before I sat down. "Maybe it should be more about the war itself. Maybe about someone like Ricky's brother, who is a war hero."

Ricky's eyes lit up. There'd been no more news about Bill since that telegram. "Oh, I don't know," he said. "I mean—yeah, he's a hero to me—but there are lots of people who are heroes during this war."

"Then we should write about all the heroes," I said.

Berta nodded like the idea was growing on her, little by little.

And—butter my biscuit—she actually said, "I like it."

CHAPTER 29

"It sounds like your sister's another hero we could write about," Ricky said when he finished reading Charlotte's letter while we took a break from the chore of cleaning the henhouse. "That girl in the iron lung could've died!"

I put the letter back in my pocket for safekeeping. "Yeah. Charlotte got in the good line, for sure."

"What good line?"

I shrugged. "You know—sometimes I imagine babies standing in lines up in heaven to get all the things they'll be born with. Charlotte must've got in the line for all the good things. She's always good. And you're right—she's definitely a hero—like your brother."

Ricky shrugged. "Hadn't thought about it that way—but yeah, Bill must've been in the good line too. I'm sure he's a hero. Don't know for certain how he got hurt, but I'll bet you anything it was helping somebody. That's just who Bill is."

He looked back at me and tipped his head like he was trying to figure something out. "So, what line would you have been in up in heaven?"

That was easy. "I got in the line for trouble. Trouble for me, trouble for everyone who knows me. Probably went back for a second helping."

He laughed at first and then stopped. "Wait. You don't really believe that you're bad luck for people, do you?"

"I don't just believe it—I know it. How else do you explain all the bad luck in my family? There has to be a reason."

Ricky shrugged. "What about me? My pa left and didn't come back—and my big brother got hurt in the war. Do you suppose that's 'cause I'm bad luck?"

"'Course not. That's just—"

"Just the way some things work out, right?" Ricky's expression was so serious. "Can't rightly give a good reason for most bad things. I think bad things just happen—sort of like accidents do."

I knew he was right about him not being bad luck, and

I remembered the circle of life thing that Granddaddy talked about. But I guess I'd just been thinking I was bad luck for so long now, it was going to take some adjustment to think differently.

* * *

The smell of warm bread greeted us as we opened the door to the house. Betsy had been excited to help Grandma with her baking, and her blue overalls were now speckled white with so much flour, I wondered how much had ended up in the bread.

But before I could say anything, I heard the sound of shattering glass in the cellar.

"What was that?" Ricky asked, but there wasn't time to answer. He and I ran down the steps to find Buster out of his crate, racing around the cellar and knocking over Grandma's canning jars like bowling pins.

"Buster, no!" I tried to stop him, but he must've thought it was a fun new game. He'd never jumped out before, and I guess he liked the feeling of being free. Ricky and I tried to catch him, but when all three of us slipped on the pickle juice and fell into a heap, we couldn't stop laughing.

"What on earth?" Grandma's voice didn't have a speck of laughter in it as she came down the stairs with Betsy trailing behind her.

I turned as serious as I could as Grandma took in the scene. "I'm sorry, Grandma. Buster's sorry."

"Out! He's going out to the barn tonight. He's too big to stay inside anymore."

"But, Grandma, he's—"

"He's a farm animal—that's what he is. And farm animals live in barns. You would do right not to forget that."

Ricky kept his arms around Buster, who smelled like a pickle now, to keep him from getting into any more trouble.

Grandma looked back at hours of her canning work now trickling across the cellar floor. She shook her head and pointed her finger at me. "I know I don't have to tell you to clean up this mess real good, now."

"No, ma'am. I mean, yes, ma'am. I will."

When Grandma shut the cellar door, Buster shook himself off, spraying pickle juice across Ricky, Betsy, and me. We tried not to laugh, but we couldn't help it.

When we finally got Buster back in his box, he bucked Ricky's hand to get him to pet his head while Betsy patted his back.

"He *is* getting pretty big." Ricky started to pet Buster as he spoke. "Whatcha feeding this guy?"

I had to admit, Buster was more than three times larger than when we first got him. "He's getting grains now, and water. He's eating a ton," I said. "I miss giving him his bottle, but my hands sure don't! All that head buckin' really hurt." I looked down at the remaining scab on my right hand from more than a week before.

And then I looked inside Buster's box, seeing—and smelling—that even more cleaning was needed.

I hated to say it, but maybe Grandma was right. Buster was too big to be inside anymore.

Ricky stopped petting Buster. "So where do we start?"

"I guess we gotta keep that clumsy guy away from one mess so I can clean up the other. Maybe you can hold him while I sweep and mop up. Betsy, could you get the bucket that's outside by the porch? I'll go get something for the broken glass."

I should've been mad at Buster for causing all this extra work, but when I looked at him, covered in pickle juice and sitting, so happy, in his box, I just couldn't muster up anything but a laugh. It *was* pretty funny.

I shook my head. Sometimes Granddaddy tells me if I'm not careful, I might find myself in a pickle. I don't think I'll ever think of that expression the same way after today.

CHAPTER 30

Buster's first night in the barn wasn't fun for him.

Or me.

Granddaddy fixed a nice pen close to our cow, Molly, but on the opposite end of those noisy pigs. I lined his pen with more straw than he could ever need, to make sure he'd be comfortable.

Ricky was there when I brought Buster over to the cow and introduced them.

"Molly, this here is Buster. He's a lamb."

Ricky laughed. "Don't ya think she knows he's a lamb without you telling her that?"

"How would I know if Granddaddy ever had any lambs before?" I looked back at Molly, who had looked away from me. Buster was starting to rub against her as she snorted and stomped her foot, ignoring him.

"See? That's what I'm talking about." I turned Molly's face back to look at me. "This here's a lamb—and I want you to take care of him. You don't have to be his mama—that's my job. But be nice to him."

Buster seemed to hear what I was saying and stopped rubbing against Molly, instead coming closer to me. I opened the gate, and Buster walked on in, sniffed around, and sat down.

"Good boy!" I said as I shut the gate. "We'll see you later."

But as I turned to walk away, Buster started to complain with a bellowing bleat. Now that he was bigger, his *bleh* had turned into a deeper *baa*.

Baa! Baa! Baa! he cried, running back and forth in his pen.

Ricky looked as sad as I felt. "Don't worry. Bet he stops crying as soon as we leave the barn."

But his sad *baa*s seemed to follow me all the way back to the house.

* * *

Halfway through supper, Grandma scolded me. "Don't be so sad-eyed at my table. That lamb is where the good Lord intended him to be—in a barn with the rest of the livestock."

"Have to agree with your grandma, Pixie," Granddaddy said. "Might be time to pull away from that lamb a bit and remember he's an animal on a farm."

"And you are a girl at my table," Grandma added, "who needs the food I spent all day preparing for you. So eat up."

"Yes, ma'am," I answered, taking a bite of the stew. But seeing as I was in a sour mood, the stew might as well have been bathwater. Grandma looked at me with such a disappointed look I feared I'd said that out loud.

We were all looking pretty glum when Daddy walked into the room, late for dinner as usual.

"I got something that'll make you happy—and it sure looks like you could use it," he said as he sat down. "Charlotte's doctor sent a telegram saying she's doing real good—walking with a bit of help."

That sure did make me happy! "Can I go see her now? Please?"

Daddy looked pained, so I figured out the answer before he spoke again. "I'm sorry, honey. Children still aren't allowed to visit."

"How is that fair? Charlotte wants to see me!"

Daddy shook his head like even he couldn't understand it.

"I wish you could go visit her too, Pixie," Granddaddy said. "Breaks my heart thinking of all the kids there . . . Hurting kids . . . in iron lungs . . . in wheelchairs . . . stuck in hospital beds."

I tried to blink away the picture of all those hurting kids, because in the middle of that picture was my sissy.

"Is Charlotte still hurting a lot?"

Daddy's voice was almost a whisper. "Yeah. She's tough, but being away so long is hard for her."

My eyes started stinging, and my lip started quivering. I couldn't even think of eating any more. "May I be excused, please?"

Grandma sighed. "Yes, you may, Pixie."

I got up from the table and ran as fast as I could to the barn.

* * *

Buster seemed perfectly fine when I walked in the barn—but as soon as he saw me, he began bleating again.

"Calm down," I whispered as I climbed over the side of the pen.

He bucked at me with his head. *Baa! Baa!*

I sat cross-legged as he plopped next to me and quieted down. "Buster, sometimes life doesn't make sense," I told him, and he looked at me like he agreed. "My mama's been gone over two years now, and my sissy's been gone for more than two hundred days." My voice cracked. "That's a lot of days that I haven't seen her. I look at her picture every day to remember what she looks like, but now I'm wonderin' if she looks like her picture anymore. Imagine that! A person not knowin' what her own sister looks like!"

I let myself have a good cry, and by the time I was all cried out, Buster was asleep beside me.

I watched as the shaft of light from the open barn door got smaller as the sun set. It was peaceful listening to Molly's occasional grunts and Buster's soft snores. I was dozing off when I heard the sound of footsteps.

"Pixie, ya in here?" Daddy carried a lantern that beamed its light on us.

"Yeah."

"Figured." He walked into the barn and sat down outside of the pen.

"Daddy," I asked, "will I ever get to see Charlotte again?"

"'Course you will."

"But you can't be certain, can you?"

"Yes, I can. As sure as I am that the sun comes up each morning, that's how sure I am that my girls are meant to grow up together."

"Two hundred days, Daddy. It's been more than two hundred days." I wiped my tears with the back of my arm. "I miss her more than anybody knows."

He leaned closer. "I know that deep-down feeling of missing somebody better than I ever wanted to. But right now, all we can do is keep everything here ready for her to come home—and pray she gets home soon. I think she will. The good Lord willin'—"

"And the creek don't rise," I finished the saying. "That's the way Charlotte and I sign our letters."

I think I saw him wink, but the beam of light from the lantern wasn't bright enough to be certain. "You girls get that expression from your mama. You're both so much like her."

I didn't know what to say. My heart felt better just hearing Daddy say I was even a bit like my mama.

I stood up and tried not to wake Buster. He snorted in his sleep but didn't open an eye.

I wrapped my hand around Daddy's as we walked back to the house, the chirp of crickets competing with the crunch of our footsteps. The air was cool and sweet-smelling. "That smell reminds me of Mama."

Daddy nodded. "Yep. The lilacs are starting to bloom. Those were her favorites."

I remembered that! And I loved the smell too.

I inhaled as deep as I could. And as tight as I held on to Daddy's hand, I think I held even tighter to an honest-to-goodness memory of my mama.

CHAPTER 31

Turned out that Buster took to sleeping in the barn as easy as he took to running in the fields. Spring was really here, and he was as excited as me to be outdoors any chance he could get. I tried to keep up with him as he ran through the orchard and zipped between the apple-blossom-filled trees, but his four legs seemed more than twice as fast as my two.

Saturday found him exploring and me busy hoeing the garden, trying my best to only dig up the weeds and not any sprouting vegetables.

At first, Grandma watched to see if I hoed right while she hung up the laundry to dry. When she'd finished hanging the laundry and giving me pointers, she went inside.

As I worked, I spied Ricky walking across the orchard,

with Betsy riding piggyback. When Buster ran to greet them, Betsy jumped off to pet him.

She giggled. "Your lamb thinks he's a dog."

"Careful, or Mud will be jealous," I said.

Ricky shook his head. "Nah, Mud can't think enough to be jealous."

I laughed, but right then Buster took off running toward the clothesline with the laundry Grandma had just finishing hanging.

"No, Buster! Get," I scolded, but he must've thought I yelled, *Run, Buster, run!* since that's what he did—smack into the sheets, knocking one of them off so it wrapped around his head. I thought he'd come to a stop, figuring how he couldn't see worth a lick, but Buster ran in circles with his head covered in the sheet, making him the funniest-looking four-legged ghost that ever there was.

Then he zigged and zagged between the apple trees, heading toward the outhouse. We ran after him, hollering for him to stop, but those legs of his moved crazy fast, especially for someone just discovering he had legs at all.

Finally, right by that smelly old outhouse, he stopped, with Grandma's sheet resting on top of him. I grabbed that sheet lickety-split and saw a big dirt stain that Grandma was sure to notice.

"Should we take it back to your grandma to wash again?" Ricky asked.

"I would," I said, "but I had my heart set on living another day."

"Can't be that bad!" Ricky laughed.

But I knew what a chore washing laundry with the wringer machine was. Grandma had to feed the wet clothes through the wringer after pulling them from the boiling water with a broom handle, and I wasn't gonna be the one to tell her she had to go and do it all over again on account of my lamb.

Instead, I went over to the water pump. With Ricky pumping the water, and Betsy holding up the half that was still clean, I could rub the ends of the sheet together enough to make that dirt spot almost disappear. As soon as it looked pretty near gone, we all carried it over to the line and hung it back up.

"Stay away from the laundry this time, Buster," I scolded, fixing the last clothespin onto the line.

"He's not listening," Betsy said. "He's eating something over there."

I followed her pointing finger to see him nibbling clover in front of the henhouse.

And that gave me a great idea.

I ran to the door and opened it wide.

There was someone Buster needed to meet.

"Come on in, Buster!"

And this time, he listened.

He ran to one hen after the other, making them fly off their roosts. *Baa!* he hollered at 'em as if they weren't already scattering to the rafters, fearing for their lives, clucking and squawking all the way. Last off her roost, of course, was Teacher, who tried to peck Buster on his nose, but he answered her peck with a bellowing *Baa!* making her fly away faster than I'd ever seen her move.

I was laughing so hard I almost forgot to get the eggs while I had the chance. "Hurry," I yelled to Ricky and Betsy. "Grab as many eggs as you can while they're flying around!"

By the time Buster had lost interest in the hens and they began to settle back in their nesting boxes, I had a basket full of more eggs than I'd ever collected before.

Once we got outside, I put the basket down by the water pump. We were still laughing when I started pumping, letting the water flow, while Ricky, Betsy, and I dipped our hands in it to scoop up a drink, splashing each other. Truth be told, we got more water all over ourselves than in our mouths.

And right then, I couldn't help but notice how good it felt hearing the sound of laughter ringing out once again on the farm.

CHAPTER 32

The next day, after church, Grandma asked Ricky and me to pick the early lettuce leaves. She showed us how to only take the bigger leaves that wrapped around the lettuce head, by pulling them down and cutting them off, giving the rest of the plant another few weeks to keep growing.

Cutting my last leaf off and stacking it with the others in the basket, I was surprised how pretty the loose lettuce looked—crisp and wavy and green.

We sat down on the grass to rest a minute from all that bending over. I could hear Betsy chasing after Buster, calling him somewhere near the barn.

Ricky picked up a piece of lettuce and took a bite, so I

did the same. Through the crunch of my chewing, I heard him ask, "Is your pa visiting Charlotte today?"

I swallowed and nodded.

Ricky must've understood I didn't want to talk too much about not being able to visit again, so he changed the subject. "Guess what?"

I shrugged. "What?"

"My ma's getting better—a lot better."

"Really?"

"Uh-huh. And . . . there's something else—got me a letter!"

I gasped. "From your brother?"

"No," he answered in all seriousness. "From the president of the United States of America."

My eyes grew bigger.

"Of course it's from my brother, nitwit!"

"Are you gonna read it to me, or do I get to read it myself?"

He wiped his hands off and put them both over his pocket. "Maybe neither."

As much as that frustrated me, I was happy figuring his joking and his mama feeling better probably meant the letter didn't have bad news in it. "You're the nitwit! Now give me that letter!"

I reached into his pocket to grab it but only got a piece of it. We both heard the sound of ripping paper. If any two people knew how important it was to take good care of letters, it was Ricky and me.

I put my hand over my mouth. "I'm sorry! Did I rip it? I'm so sorry!"

Reaching into his pocket, he held his breath as he pulled out the letter. The tightness in his face relaxed as he looked at it and exhaled. "Just the envelope ripped. The letter's okay."

I exhaled, too, and I didn't even know I'd been holding my breath. Then I waited.

Ricky looked at the letter the same way I look at each of Charlotte's letters. He held it tender in his hands, looking it up and down, like he was inspecting it. Then he handed it to me. "You can read it out loud if you want."

So I did.

Dear Ricky,

I'm sorry I got hurt. I promised you, Betsy, and especially Ma I wouldn't, but I guess it wasn't up to me. I don't really remember what happened. All I know is I was in France and we were getting ready to charge—we had the target picked out, we were waiting for the command. And the next thing I know, I'm waking up in a hospital in New York City, back in the United States of America.

I was shot in the back. Guess it didn't look good for a while. They flew me to New York on an army jet. Wish I could remember that. I was on a plane in the sky! When they sent me to France, it was by boat, and it took a long time. But when I was unconscious, they flew me on a jet. Can't believe that.

Still can't remember what happened when I got shot. The doctor here says that's normal—says stress from trauma can make you forget. One of my army buddies wrote me that he's okay today because of what I did that day. But I don't remember it none, so I can't be sure. I'm just glad he's okay. He's a good man—has a baby back home and a wife.

I get a bit stronger each day. There've been a couple of setbacks with infections and stuff. My legs are a little messed up after being shot, but the doctor says I'll be walking real soon, and if I keep getting better, I'll be home by summer.

I want to make sure I'm all better by then, and I'm working hard to make it happen.

Please give Ma and Betsy a hug for me. And your teacher.

I miss you all. I miss home. Thanks for taking
care of everyone.

Love,
Bill

I handed the letter back to him. "See, your brother *is* a hero!"

Ricky nodded as he carefully put the letter back in his pocket.

I was curious why Bill kept talking about Miss Beany, but just as I opened my mouth to ask, I heard a commotion in the barn, followed by Granddaddy's voice bellowing, "Pixie! Come get your lamb!"

We arrived in the barn to find Buster weaving in and out of Molly's legs while Granddaddy, sitting on the milking stool, tried to shoo him. Betsy tried to help by clapping her hands and calling over and over, "Here, Buster!"

The commotion made that old cow shift her weight back and forth so much, she knocked Granddaddy off the stool.

"Pixie!" Granddaddy hollered like I'd made him fall.

But I understood. "Come on, Buster," I said. "Come here!"

But right then, my lamb just plumb sat down in front of the cow.

Granddaddy righted himself on the stool again and

went back to milking Molly. "Job's easier without an audience," he declared. Buster looked at him. "Yeah—I'm talkin' 'bout you." And to prove his point, he pointed Molly's udder at Buster and squirted milk in his face. But if that was meant to scold him, Buster couldn't tell. He jumped up and came to Granddaddy with his mouth wide open.

Betsy squealed with laughter as Granddaddy chuckled and obliged Buster with a few well-aimed squirts of milk, right into his mouth. "That's enough, now. Leave some for the rest of the family."

I put Buster back in his pen, smiling at him being called a part of the family.

And looking around, I started to wonder if a family might also include more than just kin.

CHAPTER 33

"Easy now." Granddaddy was showing Betsy how to milk Molly—and Ricky and I were having fun watching. When he asked us to go bring in Horse and the plow, I figured he was just tired of having us as an audience—till he added, "It's fixin' to rain."

There wasn't a cloud in the sky, but I was learning not to doubt Granddaddy's forecasts.

Ricky wasn't as sure. "How do ya know, Mr. Johnston?"

"Well, it don't rightly smell like rain yet, but it will. This morning, both Horse and Molly here was stretchin' their necks up high and sniffin' the air. They say when horses and cows do that, it'll rain. And I can't think of a time when it wasn't proved true."

* * *

'Course in no time at all, it rained. With the animals safe in the barn, and Betsy and Ricky likewise safe back home, I sat on the porch listening to the rain ping-ping-pinging on the tin roof over my head. The animals weren't the only ones who could smell the rain now. I breathed it into my lungs as I shut my eyes.

The hum of the music coming from the radio competed with the sound of rain. I shut my eyes to the sweet sound till I heard the music stop, interrupted by a voice. I couldn't hear what the voice had said, but I plain as day heard Granddaddy holler, "Thelma!"

Even though he didn't call me, I went running just the same.

The voice on the radio continued to speak. *"The Press Association has just announced that President Roosevelt is dead. The president died of a cerebral hemorrhage. All we know so far is that the president died in Warm Springs, in Georgia."*

"Oh my," Grandma gasped, with her hand clutching her chest.

Granddaddy shook his head. "A good man. A real good man . . . It's a pity . . . what with the end of the war in sight."

The voice on the radio kept talking, but I wasn't really hearing. I stood there feeling bad that my first thought when I heard my president died was that he had the same polio that my sissy had.

That's when I heard Daddy's car coming down the lane.

More than ever, I needed to know Charlotte was okay. I ran to the front door, but before I put my hand around the doorknob, Grandma stopped me. "Don't even think about going out in this pouring rain."

Daddy stepped onto the porch and shook the rain off himself like a dog. I tried to be patient, but that was never easy for me. Especially when it had to do with my sister. "How is she?" I said. "Did she read my letter? Did she give you one for me?"

Daddy brushed the rain off his shirt. "Well, hello to you too, Pru."

"Sorry. Hi, Daddy. How is she?"

"Let your daddy get fully out of the rain before you start raining your questions on him." Grandma shook her head.

Daddy winked at me. "Let's go sit in the living room by the stove, and I'll dry off and tell y'all about it."

Once Daddy got comfortable, kneeling by the wood-stove, and Granddaddy filled him in on the president's passing, I sat down on Granddaddy's lap to wait for Daddy to speak. Grandma sat down too.

"Well, that's a shame about President Roosevelt." Daddy spoke in a sad voice.

I meant no disrespect for our dead president, but I had to ask again. "Daddy, how is Charlotte?"

"Charlotte is definitely improvin'," he told us. "She's

walkin'—with help—up to five steps at a time now. That's good. That's real good."

Daddy was saying a lot of good things, but something still worried me. "Daddy, do you think Charlotte might die now, since the president died with polio?"

"Oh, honey—no," Daddy was quick to answer. "And it sounds like the president died due to something else. I'm not thinking that at all—and you shouldn't either."

But I wasn't convinced. So when Daddy finally gave me Charlotte's letter and I went to my usual spot in our room, I couldn't open it right away. I sat there for a spell, trying to get the thought out of my mind that somebody had just died who had the exact same disease as my sissy.

Dear Pixie,

How's Buster? I can't wait to meet him. I'm doing better and really hope I'll be home soon. Can't believe I missed almost an entire school year. Thank goodness Miss Beany keeps sending work for me so I don't forget everything.

Little Nancy went home. I'm happy for her but miss having her here. Since I got polio, each day feels like I'm losing a little bit more of my life.

I miss you and Daddy and Grandma and Granddaddy, on top of missing Mama all the time. I miss her so much. I've written her lots of poems lately. Found out the hospital was named after a famous poet—so maybe that's inspiring me. But mostly I suspect missing people is what's inspiring me the most to write all my poems. That's what inspired this one:

> How can I miss you
> when you're in all that I do?
> Every tear that I cry
> I know you're crying too.
> When I feel such sadness
> I know you feel it too.
> So how can I miss you?
> But, Mama, I do.

Daddy's coming soon, and I can't wait to read your next letter. But what I really can't wait for is getting home. And I will be home soon, the good Lord willing and the creek don't rise.

Love,
Charlotte

More than ever, I missed having Charlotte home, and more than ever, I could tell she was hurting with all her missing too. I leaned against the wooden frame of her empty bed and cried and cried for us both.

CHAPTER 34

In spite of it only being early May, the sun beat down something fierce while Ricky and I walked the eggs to the grocer. Ricky was in the middle of telling me about the garden his mama and Betsy were home planting when we heard wild screams coming from the store. We ran toward the commotion, but before we even opened the door, I could pretty near tell the screams weren't bad screams. These screams sounded like somebody had found gold.

"Hallelujah!"

"It's true!"

"Praise the Lord!"

When we walked in, I saw Mr. Green, another man,

a lady, and Berta all jumping up and down, hugging on each other.

"Shh." One of them hushed the others. "I want to hear President Truman's speech." A bunch of folks were facing the radio. We walked closer to them and listened.

> *"Let us not forget, my fellow Americans, the sorrow and the heartache which today abide in the homes of so many of our neighbors—neighbors whose most priceless possession has been rendered as a sacrifice to redeem our liberty . . . If I could give you a single watchword for the coming months, that word is work, work, and more work. We must work to finish the war. Our victory is but half-won."*

The woman cried. One of the men looked like he was about to do the same. For once, I wanted Berta to talk, but she was quieter than I'd ever thought she could be.

I looked at Ricky, whose smile was about to crack his face before he spoke in a shaky voice. "Is it true? Is it over? Is the war over?"

The grocer shook Ricky's hand like he'd had something to do with it all. "Not officially, son. Not officially for us. But today there's victory in Europe. It's a matter of time for the rest."

I was happy the war was over, or almost over, and soon

all the soldiers could come home, but I wanted an announcement to come on the radio telling me polio was over and Charlotte could come home.

While they all patted each other on the back, I looked at a poster by the register. It had a picture of a woman with her sleeve rolled up and her arm bent like she was showing her muscle. The words *We Can Do It!* were written on top. Made me wish I had some of that confidence. I shook my head, not hearing someone sneak up beside me.

"You just takin' them eggs for a walk, or might ya want my daddy to buy 'em?" Berta stood next to me, laughing at her own joke. She was so dang confident all the time—I'll bet she could have posed for that poster.

I shook my head. "I didn't want to bother your daddy, what with him celebrating and all."

She looked me up and down. "Aren't you happy the war's almost over? You don't look happy."

At that moment, I was glad to see Ricky appear. 'Course, Berta was glad too. She smiled a smile that I thought was so big and forced it shouldn't be called a smile. "Hi, Ricky!" she said as she put her hand on his shoulder, like she always did. "Isn't that great news?"

Ricky grinned back at her and nodded. "It is! It sure is." They stood there smiling at each other for longer than seemed natural.

But Berta couldn't stay quiet for too long. "Maybe we should talk about this in our speech?"

I'd been surprised that over the last month, the three of us had managed to get some good thoughts down about our heroes speech. I had to admit that Berta was pretty smart—but I also had to admit she sure liked letting us know it.

Berta was talking in that voice of hers that's always telling something, never asking. "I was practicing what we have—since I know I will be the one who presents it." Ricky grinned at me while Berta kept right on talking. "But I've decided it seems a little slow . . . a little boring. I think we need to do something to make it different from everybody else's speech."

My heart was so full of missing Charlotte that my head couldn't begin to think about schoolwork right then, so I just shrugged and said, "Well, what do you want us to change? Should we do a dance? Sing a song? Maybe turn our speech into a big ole poem?"

"That's it," Berta yelled. "That's a good idea! The poem thing—not the dancing and singing thing—although I am a good singer."

I was about to tell her I was joking when Ricky added, "Yeah! A poem could be nice." He looked at me. "You know how much you like Charlotte's poems? I'll bet if we wrote a poem for part of our speech, it'd make people remember it more."

I did like Charlotte's poems. And I figured it might be nice to think of Charlotte while I was writing one of my own.

But before I could think any more about it, Ricky turned back to Berta. "But now, me and Pixie better be getting these eggs sold and the sugar her grandma needed."

I was happy to move on, so I headed to the counter. Grandma's ration book was inside the basket with the eggs. I pulled out the stamp for our allowed amount of sugar and handed both the stamp and the basket to Berta's daddy.

Mr. Green smiled a real nice smile. "Maybe before long we won't need these here ration books anymore, and people can buy any amount of anything they want."

I nodded, 'cause it seemed the polite thing to do, but truthfully, I couldn't remember when we didn't have to take the stamps and the book to the grocer with us. The idea of not doing it that way, and buying any amount you wanted, seemed strange to me.

He handed me the sugar and some change for the eggs, then winked and said, "Mark my word, everything will be back to normal one day soon."

As much as I wanted to believe yet another grown-up's promise, I had to wonder if I'd even recognize what normal looked like if it ever did decide to come back into my life again.

CHAPTER 35

It was finally the day for us to give our speeches in front of the class so that Miss Beany could choose who got to present during the pageant.

Since two of Berta's favorite things are being the center of attention and talking, Ricky and I agreed with her that she'd be the best one to give our speech.

It took a long time to put the right words into our poem, but I think we did it.

I know without a doubt the poem we came up with wasn't near as perfect as one of Charlotte's, but I thought she'd be proud she inspired it.

The first group to present gave a speech about doing our part with war rations and victory gardens—the gardens President Roosevelt, may he rest in peace, asked everyone in the country to plant. It was a pretty good speech, and so was the next one about a day in the life of a soldier in the war.

When our turn came, the three of us stood up in the front of the classroom—but Ricky and I stood off to the side holding the collection of wartime pictures we'd cut and pasted from *Life* magazine. I looked over at the lonely row of desks where I'd sat when Miss Beany wasn't 100 percent sure I wasn't gonna give the whole class polio. Hard to believe how long ago that was. And that made me sad, thinking how long ago it was since Charlotte was here.

I shook my head, trying to shoo away those gloomy thoughts, and tried to focus instead on Berta giving our speech.

"Our late president Franklin Roosevelt in his first inaugural speech said, 'The only thing we have to fear is fear itself.' But what is fear, and how does someone overcome their fear and become a hero?"

I dang near memorized that speech myself, but standing beside her, listening to her recite it to our class, I got goose bumps.

After talking about soldiers and everyday heroes of the war, she recited the poem we wrote.

There are heroes all around us,
especially in a time of war.
Some fight on the battlefield,
and some run the local store.
Heroes come in different shapes:
some are women, some are men.
Some fight for life in a hospital
so they can come home again.
There are heroes all around us
and within us all—it's true.
Because the power to be brave
also lives in me and you.

Had to admit that might have been the best speech ever.

Miss Beany liked it too. And Ricky, Berta, and I were all kind of tickled when everyone clapped for a long time.

At the end of the day, Miss Beany announced that our speech was chosen to be given during the pageant.

We squealed and hugged each other.

"That really was good." I smiled, feeling pride swelling inside me.

Ricky touched Berta on the shoulder. "You have such a good memory," he said.

And she did—she remembered every single word of our speech and poem without any papers to look off of.

Berta smiled. "I know! Daddy says I'm like an elephant—I never forget anything."

I wanted to add she also never forgets to compliment herself, but I swallowed that thought as we were enjoying the good feeling of our accomplishment.

CHAPTER 36

With the pageant only a week away, there was a lot more practice and preparation to do. Miss Beany announced that it was going to be bigger than the Fourth of July and that the whole town was invited. I think the teachers added every patriotic song ever known to the program.

I didn't mind learning extra songs the last week of school instead of doing arithmetic and spelling. But I was surprised when Miss Beany asked me to sing "God Bless America"—and extra surprised she wanted it sung as a duet with Berta.

That meant the last week of school I had homework with Berta. Of course, she insisted we practice at her house since her daddy owned a phonograph player and even had the record of that song. I'd heard it on the radio more than any other song ever sung, it seemed. But I still didn't know it by heart.

So one afternoon, I followed Berta home from school.

"Hey, girls!" Her daddy waved to us when we walked in the store. "Prudence, nice to see you. I'm glad you come over. Berta don't get a lot of friends visitin'."

"It's not really a friend visit, Mr. Green. We got homework of sorts to do."

Those words took a sliver of the smile away from her daddy's face, and I admit to feeling a smidge mean about saying it the way I did.

But Berta didn't seem to notice. She acted like she was hosting a party and I was her guest of honor. She grabbed my hand and said, "Come on—I'll show you my room. It's upstairs."

I guess I always figured she lived near the store, but I never knew she lived *in* the store. Well, if truth be told, she lived above the store. So I followed her up the stairs, right past the indoor toilet she'd been bragging about—which I had to admit looked pretty nice and didn't smell like an outhouse.

Come to find out nothing was near as fancy as I had imagined it would be. Her stairs creaked as much as the stairs at my house, and her room was no bigger than Charlotte's and mine, even though I am sure her closet had lots more clothes in it.

She wasn't at all satisfied with me not complimenting her on her room, though. Looking around like she was searching for something special, she finally found a braggable item. "See my ribbons and awards? This one is for the spelling bee last year—you weren't here then, but I won it fair and square, no matter what that Olivia says." Her face pinched up for a moment like she was hearing Olivia disagreeing with her right then, but she moved on. "And this is from my 4-H project from last summer at the county fair. I can only do cooking and sewing projects, since we don't live on a farm or anything. You're so lucky you live on a farm." After those words, she smiled one of her famous extra-big smiles.

Butter my biscuit! *Me* . . . lucky?

"Um . . . thanks," I said. "Can we practice the song now?"

"Sure," Berta said. "I was just about to say let's go into the parlor."

I wasn't certain what a parlor was or where in a house it might be located, but I followed her through a hallway with some shelves of books and then into a room that most folks would call a living room. She walked over to the corner of the room and announced, "Ta-da!" like she'd performed a magic trick.

Her phonograph was even prettier than I'd thought it would be. There was one at school, but this was nicer— maybe the nicest one ever made.

When it was shut, it looked like a fancy version of Granddaddy's radio, only made out of smooth red wood, which looked—and felt—like touching glass. But when Berta lifted the lid, I saw the phonograph part. And waiting on top of the turntable was a shiny black record.

"Do you like it?"

"It's beautiful," I said.

She nodded. "I know."

And even though that could have been bragging, it didn't bug me. It just felt like we agreed. She turned a knob and lifted the needle, and the music started.

"God bless America, land that I love . . ."

Even though I'd heard that record on the radio before, there was something about having it right there in front of me, like the lady herself was singing just for me.

Of course, the lady *and* Berta were both singing just for me, since Berta was bound and determined to let me know she knew the whole thing by heart.

Still, when I heard the last part—*"My home . . . sweet . . . home!"*—I got goose bumps again. "That was nice," I said real soft.

Berta smiled like I was talking about her singing, which was pretty good too. But I didn't need to tell her that, since she tells everybody that all the time.

"Daddy says I have my mama's voice," she said, kinda proud but also kinda sad.

And I understood. "Then your mama must've had a real pretty voice."

"Thank you," she said. "Sometimes I pretend I can hear my mama's voice. But that's silly, 'cause I wouldn't really recognize it, would I?"

I blinked a few times, trying not to get too emotional. "That's not silly. Sometimes I pretend my mama's talking to me, too—but I can't always remember her voice either."

Berta nodded so slow it almost couldn't be called nodding. Then she smiled—a real honest-to-goodness smile.

We practiced our song over and over so many times that day that I figured God would hear us high up in heaven and have no choice but to bless America and all of us soon enough.

CHAPTER 37

If a blessing was on its way to me, it rightly got sent to someone else.

The night of the pageant, I sat at the dinner table, proud of the pretty white dress with blue and red ribbons that Grandma had sewn for me. I was so excited I couldn't sit still. I practiced the song in my head, thinking how I'd end it with my hand in the air on the last note, just like I'd imagined the real singer on the record would end it.

'Course, when she was singing it, she most likely wasn't sitting at the table with a bowl of vegetable soup. And unfortunately, in my excitement about singing, my bowl tumbled smack-dab into my lap. When I stood up, my dress was more red than white.

Grandma didn't even have time to scold me about my

messiness, since we had to find another dress for me to wear right away—and seeing as how I'd grown a foot over the last few months, the pickings were slim. All that was left for me was an old gray dress that had absolutely nothing to do with America.

"Quit tugging at the dress, Prudence," Grandma said to me when I walked back into the kitchen in the too-tight dress.

"I can't help it, Grandma. I don't think I can sing in this thing. I can barely take a deep breath."

She shook her head. "Well, it's going to have to do."

She was right. We were out of time.

And to make everything even worse, just then Daddy walked into the kitchen wearing his farm clothes and announced, "That old sow's giving birth tonight—I just know it."

That got me focused on his clothes instead of mine. "Daddy, why aren't you ready?" I asked. "We have to leave in a few minutes."

He looked confused. "Ready for what?"

"Tonight's the pageant at school," I reminded him.

"Oh! Right." He shook his head. "Honey, I'm sorry—but the sow's pretty old, and she'll need help getting her litter out."

Granddaddy spoke up. "Charles, you go to the show, I'll stay."

"No. I should handle it. I need to be there."

"I think your daughter might need you more tonight." Granddaddy spoke low, like he didn't want me to hear, but I did.

Daddy shrugged and gave me a smile. "Pru—you understand, right? You'll be okay if I miss your show. Maybe you can sing your song for me later?"

I wanted Daddy there at school—watching me on that stage. But I knew the farm was important to him. "Sure . . . Daddy." I smiled back as best I could.

"Well, speaking of the show," Granddaddy said, "we'd better be getting our young star to her performance now."

I tried to smile. "Ah, Granddaddy, I'm not that good."

"I know better, Pixie." He picked up my hand as we headed to the car.

* * *

The school cafeteria was decorated in all sorts of patriotic pictures colored by the students over the last week. There was a table with red punch, and cookies cut in the shape of stars. Some of the audience sat in chairs while some stood against the walls, waiting for the pageant to start.

Right as the crowd got extra loud from everybody greeting everybody else, Principal Logan hushed us all and welcomed everyone, saying how happy he was to end the year with good news. I wasn't feeling the good news right then; mostly I was feeling the tightness of the too-small dress.

My class watched from the hallway as the first graders got things started, marching and singing "Yankee Doodle Dandy." I could see Betsy singing with them, grinning even more than usual. She couldn't take her eyes off her mama—who smiled back at her from the front row.

When the second graders were getting set up and the first graders were being seated on the floor, Betsy saw me and waved. When I lifted my arm to wave back, I heard something snap.

"Oh no," I whispered to myself, but Ricky, standing next to me, must've heard.

"Don't worry. You'll be great."

But as he said that, I heard a ripping sound. And Berta, who was standing on my other side, warned me, "Be careful. You busted two of your buttons on the back of your dress."

I stiffened my back against a wall as the third and fourth graders got called to perform "My Country 'Tis of Thee."

Somehow, my dress was getting tighter with each breath I took.

When our time came to move to the space in front of the cafeteria that was serving as our stage, I walked sideways as slow as I could, keeping my back to the wall. Berta saw me taking a place in the back row, instead of where I was supposed to be—beside her, in front. She shook her head something fierce, but I just looked away.

I didn't care—my head was throbbing like someone was hammering on it. My dress was clinging to me like skin. And I thought I smelled like soup.

Miss Beany introduced Ricky, Berta, and me as the ones who wrote the fifth-grade speech. Even in the back row, I tried to concentrate on every word of the speech while Berta gave it, but my mind kept coming back to my too-tight dress. I couldn't even enjoy the round of applause we got when she finished.

Next, we all sang "You're a Grand Old Flag." We were also supposed to march in place while singing, but I was sure my whole dress would march right off my body if I moved too much, so I just kind of swayed from side to side as careful as I could. I saw Grandma and Granddaddy nodding and smiling at me, but I sure didn't feel like nodding or smiling back.

Then it was time for Berta and me to sing our song.

Miss Beany introduced us, and Berta jumped out to stand away from her row. I went to move forward too, but when I took a breath to do so, I heard a couple more pops from what were certainly my last buttons.

I couldn't move.

Berta stood in her spot, fanning her fingers my way, motioning for me to come to her, while I shook my head, wishing I could just disappear.

She left her spot in front to come back to me, speaking in a loud whisper, "Forget about your silly buttons—we have a song to sing."

Except I couldn't say—or sing—a word.

And even though my mouth refused to work, somehow my feet managed to run me out of the cafeteria, my bare back broadcasting my shame to the entire school.

CHAPTER 38

Granddaddy and Grandma tried to tell me I didn't embarrass myself beyond repair, but I only found comfort in the fact that summer was here and I wouldn't have to see most everyone from school until the fall.

That night, I tossed and turned—and so did my brain— for what felt like hours, till I finally got out of bed. Peeking into Daddy's room, I saw him sound asleep. He must've come in after I went to bed.

Walking downstairs to Grandma and Granddaddy's room, I heard each stair creak louder than the next.

"Is Daddy mad at me?" I whispered when I got to their open door.

Grandma mumbled something and scooted over.

I took that as an invitation to sit on the edge of her bed.

Grandma's voice was little more than a whisper. "Why would your daddy be mad at ya?"

"He didn't even remember I was singing in the show, and I told him over and over. But it's more than that—it's like the only thing he cares about lately is the farm."

Granddaddy sat up in bed and put on his reading glasses, like that was gonna help him think better. "It's true your daddy's working hard on the farm," he said. "I think it's his way of dealing with everything." I looked over at him, his hair glowing silver in the moonlight. "You see, Pixie, as much as you miss your mama and your sissy, and as much as your grandma and I miss 'em, your daddy misses 'em too. But his pain might be even worse 'n ours."

I disagreed. "No way it's worse than mine. I gave Mama the cough and Sissy the polio."

"Lands' sakes!" Now Grandma sat up in bed too. "Why you keep saying that? Your mama got sick. Sometimes people get sick and get right better. Other times people get sick and don't get better. It just happens. Same with your sissy. It just happens."

I shook my head.

"Listen to your grandma," Granddaddy said. "She's right, Pixie. Nothing you did or coulda done about either your mama or sissy. But knowing how you feel, maybe you can understand your daddy a bit more."

I scooted closer to Grandma, laying my head on her shoulder like I used to do with Mama as he continued. "You see, he wanted to protect your mama and your sissy—but he couldn't. So now, working on the farm—making it better for all of us—those are things he *can* do. That's a way he *can* help. So he's holding tight to that. That's his way of pushing on."

We sat in the quiet darkness of the room for a few minutes as I tried to digest all that information about Daddy's feelings.

I squinted at the sparkling moonlight, hoping to keep my tears from falling.

After a while, I heard Granddaddy snoring, still with his glasses on. Grandma took a deep breath and patted my back. "Now, scoot up to bed—and no more silly talk. Things always look better in the light of day."

She blew me a kiss, and as I was leaving, she whispered, "To tell you the truth, your daddy is doing a great job. We needed him."

And for once, I bit my tongue, 'cause I wanted to say I needed him too.

CHAPTER 39

If I thought time with Daddy was going to make me feel better, I was just plain wrong.

A few days after the pageant, I got back from gathering the eggs, surprised to see Daddy still sitting at the breakfast table, like he was waiting for me.

The day had started out like any other summer morning on the farm, with the heat of the sun already burning my shoulders on my trek from the henhouse. Buster had given Teacher a real runaround, and I must've been smiling all the way back to the house.

But that wouldn't last.

"Daddy, you should see Buster in the henhouse, stirring up those old hens. It's so funny. I grab—"

"I need to talk to you, Pru," Daddy said. He looked serious as he patted the seat of the chair next to him.

My breath caught. "What's wrong with Charlotte?"

"Charlotte's good—I think we can actually plan on getting her home this summer."

I'd waited to hear those words for so long I squealed like one of the pigs. "That's great news, Daddy!"

I wanted to leap up 'cause my heart felt so happy, but I could see Daddy wasn't celebrating. "What's wrong, then?"

"This isn't about Charlotte, Pru—it's about Buster."

I can't be sure if it was my heart or my stomach that jumped right then, but I looked down at the table.

"Pru, do you remember when we first got Buster?"

"I'll never forget it."

"Honey, when I told you about him, do you remember me pointing out he was a farm animal—not a pet? And farm animals have jobs on the farm."

"B-Buster helps on the farm, Daddy. You should see the way he helps get the eggs, and—"

"No." Daddy shook his head. "That's not the job I meant. A livestock animal's job on the farm is to earn money by going to market. You know that was always the plan. I'm sorry if I didn't make that clearer from the beginning."

Every conversation the adults had had with me about Buster—being a *farm animal . . . livestock . . . not a pet*—came rushing back in a blur. How had my ears heard something over and over that my heart was only hearing for the first time?

Daddy went on. "Do you understand what I'm saying?"

Now my heart heard loud and clear. I knew—but I couldn't understand. How could I let Buster go? Tears rolled down my cheeks. "Isn't there a way we could keep him?"

Daddy's voice cracked. "No, honey. There isn't room for a hundred-pound pet on a working farm. Clyde was over to help deliver the piglets and checked out Buster. Said you did a right fine job with raising him. He could bring a good sum of money at market, and once we take out the feeding cost, that money's yours."

"I don't want money. I want Buster."

He put his arm around me. "I'm sorry. It's costing too much to care for him as a pet. The farm's in a place to start making better decisions, not worse. We need to make every penny count."

I wiped my eyes and looked at the coffee can of money. "But you have money in the piggy bank. Can't that go to feeding Buster? *Please?*"

"Do you think that's what would be best for our farm?"

"It's not *my* farm—but it's *my* Buster!" I couldn't look at

Daddy. "Saving Buster would be right for him and for me!"

He tried to pat my hand, but I pulled away. "It's *your* farm because it belongs to all of us. And we all have to do what's right for our farm—for our family. And I'm not saying it has to be today—"

"Today?"

"It doesn't have to be today, but it has to happen, and I think these things are best not put off too long. Sometimes it's best to get it over with."

* * *

Those words echoed in my head as I stood up. And without remembering taking steps at all, I soon found myself in the orchard.

"Buster! Buster!"

He was chasing a butterfly, but when he heard me, he came running. His head butted against my hand as I petted him. I bent down and tried to hold on to his neck, but he just wanted to be petted, not held. "I'm not gonna let you go, Buster. I won't."

Tears fell down my face and onto his wool. It was hard to deny how big he was. His coat was soft and full, like tufts of cotton stuck together. He was strong enough that he could knock me down easy if he wanted to. But he would always be my baby.

I started walking out of the orchard faster and faster, breaking into a run. Buster followed me.

Before too long, I saw Ricky's house and stopped to catch my breath.

Taking a few deep gulps of air, I squinted at his house. From far away, I thought I saw Ricky out front, but as I walked closer, I realized it was a woman who wasn't his mom.

Then I got a little closer and I saw the woman looked like Miss Beany, but her hair wasn't pulled tight into a bun. It hung soft and loose and pretty.

She heard me when I got into the yard. "Hello there, Prudence. How are you doing?" It *was* Miss Beany, but I couldn't talk.

Ricky came outside smiling, like there was nothing strange about our teacher being at his house.

"You okay, Pixie?" he asked.

I had a lot of questions about Miss Beany, but right then all I could think of was what Daddy had just said. I knelt down to hold on to Buster. Ricky knelt to pet him too.

"I'm okay." I hugged Buster, burying my face and tears in his wool.

I heard footsteps coming closer to me. "Is something wrong with Charlotte?" Miss Beany's hand was on my shoulder.

And then the tears really started flowing. And I told them.

"Not Buster! No!" Ricky looked at Buster, who looked right at him. "He's so much like a dog, I guess sometimes I forget he's a lamb."

"I loved the stories you wrote about this little guy in class. I'm sorry about what's going on now," Miss Beany said as she sat down next to us.

We all sat there petting Buster, who sat still for only a few minutes before running around Ricky's yard, eating grass and anything else growing.

From behind me, I heard barking.

Ricky laughed. "Uh-oh."

Mud circled Buster, who looked at the dog like he was the funniest-looking lamb he ever did see. Buster lowered his head like he was getting ready to charge him. Softly, he bumped him in the side, and Mud nudged him back, but in a friendly way.

They did this around the yard a while longer before Ricky turned to me. "Do you think you can talk to your pa about Buster?"

"I tried."

"Is there anything I can do to help?" Miss Beany asked.

"Can you help me hide Buster or convince Daddy he doesn't have to go to market?"

She took a breath before answering. "Town's too small for hiding much of anything. And the only other reason farms have lambs is for their wool. But you'd need more lambs for that to work, I guess. I don't know. I wish I could help."

And I knew she meant it. "Thank you."

She stood up. "Let me know if you think of something I can help with." And she headed into the house, walking in like she lived there.

Despite being sad, I was also mighty curious. I had to know what was up. "Miss Beany?" I said to Ricky. *"Here! Why?"*

"Miss Beany and Bill . . . they were high school sweethearts," Ricky explained. "But when Bill joined the army, they put getting married on hold. She didn't want me to get teased or nothing, so we didn't tell folks at school. But now—"

"What happened now?"

"Don't worry—it's good. We got a telegram that Bill's getting better—gonna be released soon. And since school's let out, Miss Beany's heading to New York to be with him. Just stopped by here to pick up a few of his things."

"He's coming . . . *home*?" That word held so much meaning for me now.

Ricky grinned and nodded. "I just wish I could go too."

"But he'll be home soon. That's what's important. And he'll be so proud of you taking care of everyone while he was gone. You did a good job, Ricky. Maybe he'll want you to keep that job even when he gets back."

He shook his head. "Nah. I'm happy Ma's better, and it'll be good to get Bill back. One thing I learned this year is being responsible's a lot of work. Too many decisions. And sometimes those decisions are just plain hard."

Right then Buster ran back into our view, with Mud chasing him. I looked up at the sky, trying to keep my eyes from misting over again, thinking sometimes those decisions aren't just hard—they're downright heartbreaking.

CHAPTER 40

Halfway across the orchard on my way home, I spied Granddaddy coming to fetch me. He turned around when we got to him, and we walked in silence the first few minutes. But eventually, I couldn't hold in my words any longer. "I can't say goodbye to Buster, Granddaddy. Can you tell Daddy there's a better way? Please?"

I heard him take a deep breath before responding. "Pixie, I've been on a farm my whole life. I can't even count how many animals I seen go to market. Remember us talking about that circle of life? That's just the way it is on a farm."

"But why? Why does it have to be that way?" I stopped walking.

He turned to face me. "Buster's a lamb—and lambs go to market 'round here. Doubt if that's ever gonna change. But I guess the decision *you* might have to make is how you want to let him go."

"What does that mean?"

"Pixie, when it's time for something or someone to leave us—and there's nothing we can do about it—we have a decision to make. We can cling to it and make it as hard as possible to push on, or we can open our arms and let it go. It still hurts, but letting go leaves fewer scars."

"I don't think I'm brave enough to let Buster go, Granddaddy."

He put his hand on my shoulder. "Hmm . . . didn't somebody help write a speech not long ago where they talked about fear and heroes?"

"Yeah—but that wasn't about me being a hero."

"What was that one part about how being brave is in everybody?" Granddaddy winked at me.

I shook my head. "I don't remember."

"Yes, you do. I saw your lips moving along with every word Berta spoke that night. Something about being brave inside?"

I breathed in, but the words weren't easy to let out. "The power . . . to be brave . . . also lives in me and you."

Granddaddy took my hand. "Wise words from a brave young lady."

But I wasn't so sure.

Maybe words are just funny that way—it's easier to write them than it is to live them.

CHAPTER 41

In one way, the day it happened seemed like a picture show playing in slow motion, lasting for hours. But in another way, those same minutes sped by like a twister, stirring up so many things that you couldn't see any of 'em clear.

"Are you okay?" Daddy's words were soft, but I wasn't finding any comfort.

"Not really," I answered, standing next to Mr. Grayson's truck. Daddy turned and hugged me.

I squinted to find Buster, who was running to the orchard, the glare of the sun burning more tears into my already-wet eyes.

Part of me hoped he'd run and just keep running. But

there he was, eating a green apple off the ground like it was any other day.

"Whenever you're ready," Daddy said.

I'd never be ready for this—but that didn't matter.

"C-c-come here, B-B- . . . Bust—!" My lips quivered too much to get it all out.

Daddy's eyes glistened. "You want me to get him?"

I shook my head. *I* needed to do this. I took a breath. "Buster!"

He heard me. And he came running. Like always.

I gave him a last hug. "I'm sorry, Buster. You're the best lamb ever."

Baa! Baa! He butted his head against my hand, which I had to hold on to, to steady it enough to pet him.

Daddy opened the tailgate of the truck, which squealed with a shrill sound, and Buster followed my lead into the truck bed. He was too busy exploring the truck for me to be able to tell him everything else I needed to tell him.

Daddy cleared his throat. "Do you wanna go with us?"

As much as I wanted to be there for Buster, I couldn't bear to. I shook my head and jumped off the truck. Daddy shut the gate, but not before I saw Buster look back at me. With his head tilted just so, the black patch in the middle of his forehead made him look like he was winking.

My heart hurt.

"It'll be okay, Pru. I'm proud of ya," Daddy said as he climbed into the truck. "Really proud of you."

I felt arms around me and heard Grandma's and Grand-daddy's voices, but I wasn't hearing any words.

In no time, the big tires of the truck kicked up clouds of dust and dirt from the lane as Daddy drove off with Buster staring at me from the back. I could only imagine how con-fused my lamb was as he watched both the farm . . . and me . . . disappear from him forever.

CHAPTER 42

What did I do?

Before the dust had settled on the lane, I let go of Grandma and Granddaddy and ran after the truck and Buster.

What did I do?

I ran faster and harder than I ever thought I could. I heard Grandma's voice hollering, but it didn't matter.

Before I knew it, I was on the main road, still running.

Tears had to be in my eyes, 'cause I couldn't see much of anything, but I don't rightly remember crying.

I just remember running as Buster and the truck disappeared from sight.

But I kept running.

I didn't know anymore if I was running to Buster or away from everything else.

Dust closed in around me as my feet moved like never before.

One mailbox along the road gave way to another as I went farther away from the farm. Somewhere along the way of running, I guess I got off the main road, 'cause I started seeing less brown of the road and more green of the field.

Then I ran some more . . . and wound up back at that creek.

That creek where Charlotte got polio.

* * *

I stopped so fast when I saw that creek that I fell down. Landed smack on my backside. And there I sat, glaring at the water like the creek was a big ole snake about to strike me and I was staring it down, daring it to do just that.

The July sun continued to shine on my skin, as if it was just a normal summer day.

But I was angry at the day, angry at the world, angry at the creek.

And most of all, I was angry at myself.

All that anger boiled inside me until it came screeching out in a scream that might've scared the devil himself, if he was listening.

"Ahhhhhh!"

I screamed at the creek and at the world, until I didn't have enough breath in me to scream anymore.

And then I sat there and tried to catch my breath.

"Are you . . . *touched*?"

The voice made me jump. And when I looked and saw Berta standing there, I wanted to scream again. I hadn't seen her since the day of the pageant, and she looked different—wearing overalls just like me.

"What are you talking about?" I asked.

She stepped farther away from me, like I might be contagious. "Screaming like that . . . Are you . . . touched in the head? That would explain a lot, I guess."

My hand clenched a handful of grass. I didn't have the strength to talk to her. "Go away," I yelled.

"I don't gotta listen to you!" she yelled right back at me. "If I want to stay at the creek, I will. And if I want to swim in it, I will."

"Go ahead," I dared her.

She shook her head, making her curled pigtails spring from side to side. She took off her shoes and rolled up her pant legs and headed straight toward the creek like she was gonna jump right in.

"What's the big deal, anyway?" she said as she walked right to the water, like she didn't have a care in the world.

"Wait!" I shouted.

She walked on to the water's edge. "I told you not to boss me!" she said.

"Don't do it! You'll get polio!"

Her right foot froze in the air above the creek for a moment before she turned and lowered it. "What in tarnation are you even talking about?"

I walked closer to her. Decided I might as well tell her. Everything else was wrong with my life. Who cared if Berta knew how bad I was.

So I told her about Charlotte and me taking the eggs to her daddy's store last summer and us stopping by the creek. I told her about Grandma's warning, and about my mistakes that had made Charlotte fall into the water.

"And that's how she got polio."

Berta squinted like she was confused.

Then she laughed. No, she squawked like Teacher when she's daring me to take her egg.

She was laughing at my sissy getting polio! And I was ready to explode. I shut my hand into a fist and swung it back. But before I could smack Berta, she stopped squawking long enough to say, "You have a funny imagination!"

All I wanted then was to get away from everything. "Forget it. Go ahead and tell everybody how bad of a sister I am. Doesn't matter. Nothin' matters now."

As I walked away, she yelled, "Wait! I'm *sorry*!"

Guess I'm getting used to people being sorry, 'cause this

time, even that word couldn't change my mind or stop my feet from moving.

Berta's mouth kept moving too. "You mean you're serious? You really think you gave her polio when she fell in this here creek?"

I walked faster until I heard splashing. Turning around, I saw that Berta, plain as day, had walked into the creek and was splashing around like a duck who'd just found out he could swim.

I ran down to the water. "Get out of there! Didn't you hear me? You'll get sick!"

She splashed the water on her face, her arms, everywhere. Without thinking, I ran into the water, grabbed her hand, and pulled her out with me, so hard we both fell down.

When we were both on the ground, I yelled, "Do you want polio?"

Berta sat up, brushing off her overalls. " 'Course I don't want the polio. But I know that creek's fine. I swim in it near every day in the summer. And I did last year too. I don't know where Charlotte got sick, but it weren't from that creek."

"Are . . . you . . . s-sure?"

"Sure as I'm sitting here."

As if I'd been holding my breath underwater for too long and finally made it up to the surface, I gasped.

The creek isn't a polio creek? I didn't give my sissy polio?

And as the reality of her words sank in more and more, I couldn't keep myself from hugging Berta. And so I did. Wet clothes and all.

"Now don't be getting all silly about it." She tried to sound like she was annoyed at my hug, but she hugged me back.

And then we sat there for a few more minutes, like we had to refocus our view of each other before we could go on.

She spoke first. "Even though you thought that water was bad, you came after me."

I guess I did. I shrugged, not sure what I could say.

She smiled. "Thanks."

I shrugged again. "It's just a creek. Nothing bad."

"But you didn't know that when you came to save me."

I took a deep breath. "Thanks for telling me it wasn't a polio creek after all."

We stayed a while longer, the summer sun fast drying our clothes.

"Is that why you screamed at the creek earlier? You thought it got your sissy sick?"

"Partly." And then I told her about Buster and the truck and me running and running. She listened and even had tears in her eyes when I was done with my telling.

"No wonder you're so mean all the time," she said.

Butter my biscuit! She said that like I should have

agreed with her or something. But I took offense at her words. "What do you mean I'm so mean? You're the one who's mean."

"I'm not mean. You are. You're the one who rolls their eyes every time I talk. You're the one thinking she's so much better than everybody. And you're the one who ran off without singing the song with me."

"I heard you sang it anyway and did good."

"But it was better with you."

Again, my brain was taking in more information than I could handle. And I still didn't understand. "But you stuck your tongue out at me. You tripped me. You—"

She looked down. "I swear I didn't trip you that time— but the other stuff . . . Okay . . . maybe I haven't always been nice to you. I'm sorry. Maybe . . . just maybe . . . I was a little jealous of you."

"Of me?"

"Yeah—you're so . . . sure of yourself. You don't care what anyone thinks. And Ricky likes you so much."

That was more than one body could take in for one day. My heart was busy hurting over Buster, while it was still healing over not causing Charlotte's polio. My head was busy processing that Berta—confident, show-off-y Berta— was somehow jealous of *me*.

It was all too much, and none of it made sense. I was wrong about Berta. I was wrong about Charlotte. I was wrong about keeping Buster safe. I didn't know what was right anymore.

When we'd finished talking, she said her daddy could drive me home. And as much as I didn't want to be home without Buster, I guess I knew I had to go back sometime.

CHAPTER 43

Granddaddy thanked Berta's daddy kindly for bringing me back.

I figured I might get a talking-to for running away like I did, but neither Granddaddy nor Grandma said anything except I should eat something.

Instead, I headed to the barn.

I sat cross-legged in Buster's empty pen. The little bit of joy that was growing in my heart from finding out I didn't give Charlotte polio got drowned quick by the sorrow of missing my lamb.

Not sure how long I sat there before Granddaddy came into the barn, walking over to me. He sat down with a grunt on the hay bale beside the pen.

Granddaddy always had something smart to say about life being stupid. So I waited.

Nothing came.

I glanced at him to make sure he was still there. He was. Just sitting there like that was his job. "Aren't you gonna tell me I shouldn't've run away like that? Aren't you gonna tell me how I gotta be brave? That I shouldn't be sitting here wishing everything was different?"

"Reckon I don't have to tell you nothing right now."

"Good. 'Cause you could talk from today till there was no more tomorrows and I wouldn't listen. I thought I could be brave—but I'm not."

"Mm-hmm."

"Now, aren't you gonna tell me letting Buster go was the right thing to do?"

Granddaddy smiled but shook his head.

"Well, that's good. 'Cause I don't want to hear it. I thought I could let him go. But now I don't feel so brave."

"Mm . . . hmm."

"Stop saying 'Mm-hmm'! Tell me something that will make my heart stop hurting, Granddaddy. Tell me something." I got out of the pen and ran to Granddaddy's lap. He held me tight.

Finally, he spoke soft words in a deep voice. "Pixie—I want you to remember two things: First, that lamb would've

211

died when he was two weeks old if you didn't take him in. You gave him a good life full of belly rubs, bottle feedings, and more love than any lamb ever knew. You did right by him—don't be forgetting that."

I tried to nod, but I couldn't.

"And second, I can't promise your heart will stop hurting today, but I promise it will one day, the good Lord willin'—"

"Don't say it, Granddaddy. Don't say it."

He held me for a few more minutes until a shadow at the door blocked the sun's rays on us.

Ricky.

"Your grandma just told me, Pixie. I'm sorry."

I squeezed Granddaddy one more time before standing up to go to Ricky. Without a word between us, we started walking toward the orchard.

Ricky kicked a green apple as he walked. I picked up a big stick and started batting the apple away from him like we'd done before, but it wasn't at all fun.

Even without us talking, I suspected we were sharing the same thought.

We stopped near a tree with a low branch that was perfect for sitting, and both climbed on. From the lane came the crunch of gravel under Granddaddy's car. I squinted to see Daddy get out, look around, and head to the barn.

Guess he already returned the truck.

Guess he already . . .

I sighed.

My back leaned against the rough bark of the apple tree while Ricky balanced on the hanging limb, finally breaking our silence. "Seems weird. Him not bein' here, I mean. It's weird, isn't it?"

I sniffed. "Yeah."

"Remember when you first got him and he was sick right after? Remember that bath when he splashed water everywhere but fell asleep feelin' better?"

I couldn't tell if Ricky was trying to make me—or himself—feel better, remembering things we knew we'd never forget. But it was nice of him, nonetheless.

And with him being such a good friend and all, I felt bad there was ever a time I thought he was less than who he really was. So I confessed. "You know, I used to call you Rotten Ricky—can you believe that?"

He laughed. "I figured you had names for lots of people, so it don't surprise me none to find out you had one for me. Why'd you call me rotten, though? I'm not mean."

I laughed at him not remembering. "What about things like letting a frog loose in school? Or that spit wad you threw at me?"

He gasped. "I never!"

"Yes, you did. I know it."

"I swear. Okay, yeah, I brought a frog to school, but

only 'cause I found it half dead in front of the school that day and I wanted to help it. Not my fault it got out of my desk before lunch and jumped on Olivia. But that spit wad—that was *not* me."

"But when I looked up, you were looking right at me. Why else would you be lookin'?"

"I don't know. Maybe I just . . . thought . . . you needed a friend," Ricky told me. "Was that why you pushed me down after I opened the closet and let you out?"

"Yeah. And I'm real sorry about that. I thought for sure it was you." I shook my head. "Guess I don't know what's right and what's wrong anymore. And while I'm confessing—you know who else I was kinda wrong about?"

"Who?"

"Big-Mouth . . . I mean . . . Berta."

Ricky snorted. "Really? You could knock me down with a feather!" He laughed.

"I mean, don't get me wrong—she still has a pretty big mouth she likes to use. But now I see another side of her too."

Ricky shook his head in surprise. "I tried to tell ya she wasn't too bad. I admit she's kind of . . . *forceful* . . . sometimes, but she can be nice. Bet you didn't even know she told everybody you were a better singer than her."

I didn't.

I shut my eyes and tried to clear my head. Did I know anything true about anybody at all?

CHAPTER 44

It was another hard-to-sleep night. The moon shone through my bedroom window, and I looked up at the sky, wondering what Mama would have thought about today.

When Charlotte got polio, I wondered if it would've been different if Mama was here.

And now I was wondering if Buster would still be here if Mama was too.

Even if all of that would be the same, maybe it just wouldn't hurt so much if Mama was here.

Guess when you can't hang on to your mama, you hang on to your wonderings. And right then, I was holding on to my wonderings so tight I didn't hear somebody walk into the room.

"You okay, Pixie?" I didn't have to turn around to know Grandma was checking on me.

I tried to keep my voice from shaking. "Remember when I pumped my legs so high I fell outta the tire swing and landed on my hands and knees—got them scraped up and bloodied?"

"Sure do."

"Right before my scabs healed up, I fell again—running down the lane. You said the scab didn't have time to heal right proper and it broke open too soon. Left me with a scar."

I heard her footsteps coming closer.

"That's my heart right now, Grandma. Before the wound could heal from Mama dying, it got ripped open when Charlotte got sick. And now, right when it started healin' again, it's ripped all over. I don't think it's ever gonna heal."

She touched my shoulder. "If I recollect, you're pretty proud of the scars you have on your knees. You're proud of 'em 'cause you remember the fun you had before you got hurt—not the pain in fallin'. Maybe your heart's like that. You'll have your scars there forever, but instead of just remembering the pain when you count 'em, you'll think of the good times too."

Grandma rubbed my back. "Let's try to sleep. Your heart's too broke right now for words to sink in. But tomorrow, I'll tell you a little story. Remember, things always look better in the light of day."

With that, she tucked me into bed and kissed my fore-head. And though I figured I'd never sleep again, I was wrong.

CHAPTER 45

I woke to the smell of hotcakes, which Grandma usually only makes for special occasions. My birthday wasn't for another month, so I knew she was plain-as-day trying to make me feel better.

When I made it downstairs, I sat slumped in front of a stack of hotcakes, watching the maple syrup drip down each one.

Grandma pulled up a chair and sat next to me. "I remember my first lamb that had to go to market."

Now I sat up straight. "You do?"

"You never forget something like that. Name was Oscar." She smiled when she said his name. "What a rascal! Woo-wee! Always gettin' into trouble. Diggin' up the garden, runnin' through the clothesline"—she winked at me—"like somebody else we know."

My mouth opened in surprise as she continued. "Yeah, Oscar was my buddy. And then one day, he had to go."

"Didn't it break your heart?"

"Sure enough did. Plumb broke it in two. Said I'd never get me another lamb ever again. And I didn't. Till I eventually did."

"You got another one?"

"I did. Had me many lambs over the years."

"Did they all end up . . . you know . . . ?"

"Most of 'em did. We lived on a farm. Couldn't change that."

"Did they all hurt your heart . . . to say goodbye?"

She smiled and looked up, remembering. "Yeah—but nothing like that first one. Nothing like Oscar."

"I never want to see another lamb again."

"Maybe you won't. Maybe you will . . ." She patted my hand and then left hers on top of mine for a minute.

Then Grandma got up and announced, "All I can tell you about the future right now is that I made hotcakes that won't be staying hot—and if somebody don't eat 'em soon, the pigs are gonna get a mighty good breakfast today."

* * *

After I ate the hotcakes, Grandma reminded me that staying busy would be a good thing, which meant it was time for me to do my chores.

I finished gathering the eggs, and for once Teacher didn't squawk at me or puff up at all. Maybe she missed Buster too.

Then I hung the laundry on the line. With each sheet and every clothespin, I wished Buster was there to knock down the sheets and make me chase him.

Just as I was hanging the last sheet on the line, I heard a car coming down the lane. I squinted and saw it was Daddy.

And there was someone sitting in the passenger seat.

Daddy stopped the car, got out, and walked around to open the door.

My heart beat so fast I could feel it in my throat as I walked closer.

The sun was shining so bright I had to put my hand over my eyes to make sure the glare wasn't playing tricks on me.

That's when I saw the best thing I could ever see: my daddy standing right beside . . . *my sissy*.

Her arms were holding up her body with a couple of crutches, and metal braces supported her legs. But I never saw her looking better before in my life!

I ran like nothing could stop me. "Sissy!"

As soon as I reached her, I had to catch my breath in order to ask, "Would it hurt you if I hugged you?"

"I reckon it'd hurt me if you didn't." Her voice was weaker, but just as I remembered.

With tears flooding both our faces, I held on to my sissy, not sure I'd ever let her go. I breathed in the scent of her, and it felt like something in me was cracking open as so many memories rushed back. I held on to her and the moment as long as I could, only releasing her long enough to put my hand on top of hers, which rested on her crutch. Her hand was soft and cool under mine. And it had never felt better.

I turned to Daddy. "You didn't tell me!"

Tears filled his eyes. "I didn't want to risk another disappointment for you—just in case the doctor changed his mind."

By now both Granddaddy and Grandma stood next to the car too.

Holding Charlotte's hand, I just couldn't hold on to my broken heart anymore. I still missed Buster something fierce, but for the first time in a long time, I had hope—honest-to-goodness hope.

Finally, I let go of Charlotte's hand so I could give Daddy a hug. I think his arms held me tighter than they'd ever held me before.

Granddaddy and Grandma both hugged Charlotte

before Grandma scolded everyone by saying, "Lands' sakes! We gonna keep this child, fresh out of the hospital, standing in the lane all day long? Or might we get her inside like civilized people?"

Charlotte smiled. "Grandma, I missed you too." And then she laughed a laugh that sounded better to me than any song I'd ever heard.

CHAPTER 46

"Now, Charles, be careful," Grandma hollered out the window as Daddy pushed Charlotte in the wheelbarrow, heading toward the orchard. "She's just home from the hospital a week. If that thing tips over . . ." But even Grandma's worries couldn't overshadow the happiness that seemed to glow from that wheelbarrow.

I sat on the porch steps watching Daddy zip through the orchard and listening to Charlotte laugh when they scared a rabbit trying to nap in the nook of a tree. I worked hard to plant it all in my memory—the warm heat on the porch step, a dove cooing somewhere in the fields, that look on my sissy's face—I needed to store it all deep down.

I was so caught up in cementing my memories, I was

surprised when Granddaddy sat next to me. "That's a sight for sore eyes, isn't it?"

I nodded.

Granddaddy leaned closer to me, like he was going to tell me a secret, even though we were the only two people on the porch. "Just heard an interesting story."

I turned to him. "What?"

"This here story was about a certain girl who had a lamb she loved a lot—but when her daddy gave her the money she earned from raising it, she took that money and put it smack-dab in that coffee can on the counter. Did I hear that right?"

My eyes stung a bit at the mention of Buster, but I took a deep breath and nodded. "You heard right."

"What made you do that, honey? It was *your* money."

I nodded. "I know that money was my money, Granddaddy. But I also know the piggy bank money is for . . . *our* farm."

Granddaddy's eyes sparkled. "You're something else, Pixie."

I leaned against him, and together we listened to the sweet sound of Charlotte's and Daddy's laughter.

But I was also trying to figure something out.

By the time I spoke, I had to clear my throat so my words could be heard over my emotion. "Granddaddy, do you remember when you told me every day's a lesson in beginnings and endings—the circle of life thing?"

He nodded. "Sure do."

"You said life was funny that way—but I said life was downright mean."

He turned to face me. "Reckon I remember that too." Then, smiling, he added, "Still think that?"

"I don't know. I still don't like endings. But sometimes . . . if I focus on the beginnings enough, I can start to see life's not so mean after all—at least not all the time."

Granddaddy nodded slow, and I could tell he was really thinking about what I said. Finally, he spoke. "I get that. It's natural to not like endings—especially the life-changing ones. It's okay to be sad about what we've lost—as long as we don't get so caught up in our feelings for the ending that we forget to look for the new beginning. And we know that to do that, we have to—"

"Push on," I said.

He winked. "Push on."

At that, the screen door squeaked open, and I looked up to see Grandma holding the egg basket. "Pixie, could you fetch me some more eggs? I'm making angel food cake."

Since I knew angel food cake was Charlotte's favorite dessert—and maybe one of mine too—I didn't even mind visiting the hens for a second time that day. I headed to the henhouse, where Ricky was finishing up the new addition with the hatchery, which meant a rooster would be joining us soon.

"Looks good," I told him as he sanded down the new section of the coop.

He smiled. "And it sure *sounds* good out there in the orchard. So glad Charlotte's home."

I nodded. "It's the best." He followed me into the henhouse, where the rest of his tools were sitting by another new row of nesting boxes. "Any word from Miss Beany—or Bill?"

"Miss Beany—or *Adelaide*."

I giggled and shook my head. I just couldn't think of my teacher having a boyfriend—*or* a first name.

Ricky grinned and went on. "Adelaide sent us a telegram saying she made it to New York City just fine. Promised they'd both be back where they belong soon."

It was so hot in there, sweat was beading up on Ricky's forehead. And the smell of the hens was even worse when warmed by the summer heat. Still, right then I felt a cool happiness inside that didn't seem to belong in the stinky henhouse. I think Ricky felt it too.

"Is there a party in here?"

Charlotte stood at the doorway, leaning on her crutches.

Seeing her back where she belonged, the smile on my face got bigger. "You can't tell me you honest-to-goodness missed *this*, can you?"

I wasn't sure if her eyes were sparkling due to tears or just plain being happy when she answered, "You have no idea how much."

I started to tell her I had a pretty good idea, but before I could say anything, my sissy walked over to Teacher, leaned against the nesting box for support, and balanced herself so she could let go of her crutches. And right there, in that special way that only she could, she put one firm hand on Teacher's head and reached under that old hen with her other hand, grabbing the egg like no day had passed with her not being able to do that very thing.

And while I'm pretty sure neither of us would forget all the painful days that had passed since she last stood there with me like that, it didn't really matter.

All that *really* mattered was that we were, indeed, back where we belonged. Where we planned to stay—with that mean old hen and all.

The good Lord willin' and the creek don't rise.

ACKNOWLEDGMENTS

To my amazing agent, Steven Chudney, for always pushing me to be the writer I hope to be. Thank you for your wise guidance in this career I once only dreamed of.

To Nancy Paulsen. Your superpowers of publishing are legendary. I would be grateful to simply read a book you found worthy. But to be able to call you my editor once again on this, our second middle-grade novel, is a gift. Thank you to you, your wise associate, Sara LaFleur, and all the other skilled and incredibly kind people who worked on this book.

To my writing "twin," Laura Smith, for every draft you are willing to read and every comment you are thoughtful enough to give, I thank you. But more than that, I thank you for being the type of friend we all need and want to be.

Special thanks to all the teachers and librarians who get books into the hungry hands of readers. Truthfully, *thank you* isn't enough for the job you do. I just hope you have a sneaky feeling about how awesome you are and how very much you are appreciated.

Thank you to my wonderful family and friends, both in person and online, who helped fill in the missing pieces of farm life in the 1940s for me, especially after my dad passed. Your details helped me see this place like I lived there.

Thank you to my incredible (adult) kids, Megan, Katey, Scott, Ryan, and Evan. Having a book come out into the world is magical and amazing and wonderful. But watching all *your* dreams take shape and begin to fly in this world is a blessing that brings me even more joy.

To my husband, Brad, thank you for walking this publishing journey with me—as well as this journey called life. There's no one on this great big earth I'd rather walk this walk with.

And to my first storyteller, my mom, Joan McNutt, who told me the heartbreaking tale of her very own special lamb named Buster when I was growing up. Thank you for allowing me to share a piece of your childhood with the world.

Finally, to my dad, Tom McNutt—I will forever treasure the precious hours we passed in your hospital room as you and Mom recalled and revisited the farms of your youths. Though you are no longer here in person, you will live on in the details of my written words and, most importantly, forever in my heart.